Naked Bodies ~~Wouldn't Bother~~ Seely. Tenderness Would.

The time would come when I wanted her feelings as naked as the rest of her, but not yet. Not today. I touched her cheek and promised silently I would treasure and protect whatever she shared with me. Her body, for now.

Her eyes closed. "You are a devious man," she whispered.

I nodded. "You feel like rose petals."

She sucked in her breath. Her fingers fretted my hair, skimmed my jaw. She made a pleased sound, then after a moment said, "As your medical attendant, I insist that you get off your feet. Quickly."

"Want to play doctor, do you?"

"Yes." She threaded her fingers through my hair and kissed me. "And the doctor will see you now." Her hands went to the snap on my jeans.

"All of you."

Dear Reader,

Welcome to another fabulous month at Silhouette Desire, where we offer you the best in passionate, powerful and provocative love stories. You'll want to delve right in to our latest DYNASTIES: THE DANFORTHS title with Anne Marie Winston's highly dramatic *The Enemy's Daughter*—you'll never guess who the latest Danforth bachelor has gotten involved with! And the steam continues to rise when Annette Broadrick returns to the Desire line with a brand-new series, THE CRENSHAWS OF TEXAS. These four handsome brothers will leave you breathless, right from the first title, *Branded*.

Read a Silhouette Desire novel from *his* point of view in our new promotion MANTALK. Eileen Wilks continues this series with her highly innovative and intensely emotional story *Meeting at Midnight*. Kristi Gold continues her series THE ROYAL WAGER with another confirmed bachelor about to meet his match in *Unmasking the Maverick Prince*. How comfortable can *A Bed of Sand* be? Well, honey, if you're lying on it with the hero of Laura Wright's latest novel…who cares! And the always enjoyable Roxanne St. Claire, whom *Publishers Weekly* calls "an author who's on the fast track to making her name a household one," is scorching up the pages with *The Fire Still Burns*.

Happy reading,

Melissa Jeglinski

Melissa Jeglinski
Senior Editor, Silhouette Desire

Please address questions and book requests to:
Silhouette Reader Service
U.S.: 3010 Walden Ave., P.O. Box 1325, Buffalo, NY 14269
Canadian: P.O. Box 609, Fort Erie, Ont. L2A 5X3

MEETING AT MIDNIGHT

EILEEN WILKS

Published by Silhouette Books
America's Publisher of Contemporary Romance

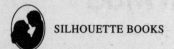 SILHOUETTE BOOKS

ISBN 0-373-76605-X

MEETING AT MIDNIGHT

Copyright © 2004 by Eileen Wilks

This edition published by arrangement with Harlequin Books S.A.

® and TM are trademarks of Harlequin Books S.A., used under license.
Trademarks indicated with ® are registered in the United States Patent
and Trademark Office, the Canadian Trade Marks Office and in other
countries.

Visit Silhouette Books at www.eHarlequin.com

Printed in U.S.A.

EILEEN WILKS

is a fifth-generation Texan. Her great-great-grandmother came to Texas in a covered wagon shortly after the end of the Civil War—excuse us, the War Between the States. But she's not a full-blooded Texan. Right after another war, her Texan father fell for a Yankee woman. This obviously mismatched pair proceeded to travel to nine cities in three countries in the first twenty years of their marriage, raising two kids and innumerable dogs and cats along the way. For the next twenty years they stayed put, back home in Texas again—and still together.

Eileen figures her professional career matches her nomadic upbringing, since she's tried everything from drafting to a brief stint as a ranch hand—raising two children and any number of cats and dogs along the way. Not until she started writing did she "stay put," because that's when she knew she'd come home. Readers can write to her at P.O. Box 4612, Midland, TX 79704-4612.

This book is dedicated to my editor, Mary-Theresa Hussey, who is as extraordinary in her own way as the story's heroine. At its best, the writer-editor relationship is a partnership that deepens over time, resulting in stronger, richer stories. I've been lucky. I've worked with the best.

One

I wasn't thinking about dying. I wasn't thinking much at all, this being one of those nights when a man didn't want to listen to the noise in his head. I'd turned the radio up loud in an effort to drown out any stray thoughts, but that may have been a mistake.

Damned country music. Every other song was about loving and losing. So why did I keep listening to it?

I grimaced and drummed my fingers on the steering wheel. The wipers were slapping sleet along with rain from the windshield, and the wind was blowing hard. But I knew this road almost as well as I knew my own street. And I'd lived there all my life.

All my life…forty years now. Most of those years I hadn't lived in the big old house alone, but I was alone there now. Forty years old and alone.

And getting dumber instead of smarter, apparently. I

scowled at the strip of highway pinned by my truck's head-lights. Why had I let Sorenson talk me into hanging around for a drink after we shook on the deal? I wasn't a complete idiot, though. Despite Sorenson's good-ol'-boy bonhomie, I'd limited myself to a single drink.

"Come on, have another one," the resort owner had urged. "On the house." He'd tried to make out that the weather wasn't a problem. We hadn't even had a freeze yet.

Yet being the operative word. I'd held on to tact by the skin of my teeth—the man was a jerk, but he was the jerk who'd just agreed to use my company for a major renovation job.

"Hey, a man your size ought to be able to handle his liquor. You don't want me to think you're a wimp, right? Might start wondering if you're man enough for the job."

I'd just looked at him, bored beyond courtesy. "Anyone who has to drink to prove he's a man isn't one."

I snorted, remembering that conversation. Yeah, I was some kind of man, all right. The stupid kind. The temperature was hovering just above freezing, visibility sucked, I had to be at a site at seven-thirty tomorrow morning and here I was, winding my way down a mountain road at ten minutes before midnight.

A sharp turn loomed. No shoulder along here. I took my foot off the accelerator and tapped the brakes. I intended to creep around that turn like an old man with palsy—an atti-tude reinforced when I saw the sign about guard-rail damage.

I hit ice halfway through.

My wheels were cut to the left, but me and half a ton of pickup kept sliding forward. The tops of a couple of pines whipped around in the wind behind the guard rails. Their roots would be thirty or forty feet below the parts I could see and beyond their roots would be a whole lot more down. I turned into the skid, then almost immediately straightened the wheel.

It worked. The rear end skated around a bit, but I'd re-claimed control. I rounded the treacherous curve, safe and sound. And through the murk of rain and sleet saw a long black whip snapping through the air. Straight at me.

A power cable. Live.

If I'd had time to think, I might have risked it. Or maybe not. The truck was grounded, but the cable might have busted my windshield and smacked me in the face with 13,600 volts. But there wasn't time then for thought, or even fear. Just action. I jerked the wheel left and hit the brakes.

Big mistake.

The truck began to spin, slick as greased Teflon. I yanked my foot off the brakes. The power cable reached the end of its arc a foot short of my bumper. I steered into the spin, more than willing to turn all the way around and head back the way I'd come.

The damned truck just kept sliding sideways.

The guard rails. I hadn't seen any damage. Maybe—

The rear of the truck thudded up against them. And stopped. The front slewed around. Jolted. And kept on going.

Even then I didn't think about dying. Didn't think at all, just flung the door open, responding to the screaming need to get out of there. But it was too late, too late to do anything but topple with the truck as it went over the edge and flipped.

Metal screeched. I turned into an object trying to bounce off the crumpling trap of the truck's cab. It was as if the dark-ness itself pummeled me with a giant's fist, and then a hard blow on my head—then silence. Stillness. I lay beneath a whole mountain of hurt listening to someone moan.

That irritated me. What business did this bozo have moan-ing when I was the one with the mountain on me? I opened my mouth to tell him to shut up. The moaning stopped.

Something in that cause-and-effect sequence woke a few brain cells. That had been *me* moaning, and I was…I was…in my truck. Only I was hanging at a funny angle.

I blinked. My right eyelid felt gummy. Slowly I put together the pressure across my pelvis and chest, the glow of the dash lights and the stillness. The nose of the truck was pointed down, but the pitch wasn't too steep.

I was alive. And I was hurt.

How bad? I couldn't tell. The pain itself addled me, made it hard to think. But my head…yeah, I remembered getting hit there. Instinctively I lifted my hand to see what touch could tell me. My shoulder exploded. Pain nearly sucked me down. I lay draped over my seat belt and shoulder harness and panted.

Okay, obviously my shoulder was hurt, too. Pretty bad.

Over the soft sound of rain I heard a creaking sound. A prickle of alarm made me lift my head. And rap it against something.

It didn't take long for me to run out of breath for cursing. Or to figure out the problem: the roof of the truck was caved in. I couldn't straighten my head.

My breath came faster. Slowly I turned my head to the right. Shards of glass glittered on the seat beside me. I couldn't see outside because light turned the starred surface of the glass opaque.

How about that. The headlights were still on. I looked to the left.

The door was bashed in.

Deep breaths, I told myself. Panic won't help. I wiggled the fingers on my left hand, then cautiously moved that arm. All right so far. With equal care I shifted my legs. Okay, good. I had three out of four limbs operational. I'd survived a tumble down a mountain and I was hurt, but I was alive, dammit. And I wasn't trapped. I could get out.

Getting out was a bitch.

The buckle to the seat belt was slippery and wet, but I got it undone, then needed to get my breath. Which was ridiculous, of course, but…my jeans were soaked. My jacket, too. And beneath the jacket my shirt stuck to me, warm and wet.

An awful lot of my blood was outside of me instead of inside.

That scared me. I reached for the door handle. My first tug didn't do a damned thing.

Fear hit, sweeping everything else out of the way. Pain didn't matter. Nothing mattered but getting out. I jerked on the handle as hard as I could, throwing my weight against it.

Metal shrieked. The door swung open and I fell out. I managed to thrust one leg out to catch myself, but the jolt as my foot hit the ground set off a charge in my shoulder that toppled my whole system.

I didn't black out. Quite. But for a while there was nothing but a red, roaring monster eating my thoughts before they could form. Eventually I noticed how cold and wet the ground was. It was a lot colder out here than in the truck. Wetter, too. Maybe getting out hadn't been such a great move, but I was here now. What came next?

The road. I had to get to the road. Not much traffic this time of night, but sooner or later that downed power line would attract attention.

Dragging myself to a sitting position left me clammy, but I made it and looked up the way the truck and I had come. Only I couldn't see the road. Too dark, and the rain didn't help. How far had I fallen?

I fought back a wave of despair. I knew where the road was—*up*. So that's where I would go.

First I used my left hand to tuck my right one into the

pocket of my jacket. There were trees, mostly pines. Not much in the way of underbrush, and the truck's passage had cleared a path through what did exist. Good. In a battle between me and a clump of weeds right then, the weeds would win.

Standing was out, so hand-and-knees it was. I started moving.

Gwen had once told me that women forget how much childbirth hurts. She made a joke of it, saying that was how nature tricked them into a repeat performance. I didn't understand then. I'd heard women swapping war stories, and it seemed to me they remembered labor pretty well.

Now I know what she meant. I remember that I hurt. Every inch up that slope equaled a yard or two of pain. But the pain itself isn't there anymore, just the imprint it left behind.

When you hurt enough, you lose hold of past and future. Like a baby or a beast, all you have is right now. I lost the knack of connecting all those nows in the usual way, like beads on a string. So some beads got lost. Others stayed stuck inside me, like a splinter the flesh has grown up around.

One of the beads that got stuck was the moment my truck finished falling.

I hadn't thought about what halted the truck's fall. Maybe that knowledge had squirmed around underneath, and that's why the creaking sound had alarmed me, why I'd been so frantic to get out. The second I heard that sharp, wooden *crack*, I knew what it meant. I craned my head to look behind me.

Branches snapped. Glass broke, and the headlights went out at last. A tangled mass of truck and tree, their shapes merged by darkness and disaster, toppled slowly, then crashed its way down the mountain. I blinked, swaying on my knees and one good hand like a suspension bridge in the wind.

That had been a damned fine truck.

I didn't mourn for long, though. I wasn't holding on to thoughts too well by then—they blew through my mind like smoke. But I had a good grip on purpose.

Up. I had to keep going up.

I remember being racked with shudders as the cold worked its way inside. At some point the shuddering stopped, but by then I was too far gone to realize what a bad sign that was. I remember thinking about Zach, but that isn't tied to any one moment. Thoughts of my son are woven through all the memory bits, like the rocks. They were everywhere, too.

I remember the angel.

That part has a beginning, a middle and an end, beads lined up neatly in order. It was the warmth that called me back. It wormed its way deep inside and tugged at me, made me notice it. And with that noticing came a thought, sluggish but complete: the warmth was real. I knew that because I started shivering again, and shivering—any movement—hurt.

I blinked open my eyes.

It wasn't her face that gave me the idea she was an angel. She was beautiful, but more exotic than angelic with her flat, wide cheekbones and tilty eyes. Her mouth was downright lush. But she had to be an angel. She was glowing.

Deeply disappointed, I croaked, "I'm dead, then."

Those full lips twitched. "No, not at all." She had a smooth sort of voice, sweet and thick like honey. And a Southern accent, which struck me as odd for an angel. "You're going to be fine."

That seemed unlikely, but even less likely things were happening right before my eyes. "You're glowing."

"I have a flashlight."

"No, it's you."

"You're imagining things. In fact, I suspect you imagined

this whole conversation." She touched my forehead. The delicate bracelet on her wrist brushed my skin, its tiny jewels winking at me. "Now, don't be wasting all I've spent on you. Go back to sleep."

I wanted to argue, but my eyes obeyed her instead of me and drifted shut. I floated away on a warm tide.

"Color's bad. Rapid respiration."

Male voices. Hands messing with me. Where was my angel?

"Nail beds are white, but it's damned cold and he's been here awhile."

"Distal pulse?"

"Can't find it."

I knew that voice. "Pete," I said, or thought I did. It came out a groan. I made a huge effort and opened my eyes. Pete Aguilar's face hovered over mine. Pete used to raise hell with my brother Charlie, but that was a long time ago. High school stuff. These days he…I blinked, trying to think of why Pete would be holding my hand.

"You with us?" He squeezed my shoulder—the left one, thank God. "Hang in there, buddy."

Oh, yeah. "Paramedic."

"That's right. Me and Joe are going to take care of you. Where do you hurt?"

Everywhere. I felt sick, dizzy, scared. "Where is she?"

"I need to know where you hurt, Ben."

"Shoulder. Head. I want…" I tried to sit up, but didn't accomplish much.

"Whoa. Stay still, or you'll open up that shoulder again."

"Dammit, I want to know—"

"I'm right here." That was her voice—close, but not as close as she had been. "Lie still and let them help you."

It's not as if I had a choice. Pete or the other man tipped me on my side. I would have belted him if I'd been able to move. As it was, I barely had the breath to curse them once they settled me on my back again.

There was something between me and the mud now. A stretcher, I guess.

"You're a lucky man," Pete told me cheerfully.

Damned idiot always had been too happy for good sense. Just like Charlie. "Not lucky...fall off mountain."

"But if you're going to fall off one, it's nice to do it just before someone with paramedic training happens along. She kept you going until we got here."

Not an angel. A paramedic. No, wait—paramedics don't glow.

A thought slipped in amidst my confusion. "Tell them... power line down. Dangerous."

"One of Highpoint's finest is keeping on eye on things until a crew arrives. Now, we've got to get you up to the ambulance where we can give you some oxygen, get a drip going. You'll feel better then."

The other man had been busy with straps. The one he fastened around my chest pulled on my shoulder. I was just getting my breath back when Pete said, "Ready? On the count of three. One...two—"

They lifted. I guess there was no way to do that without jarring me. I managed to hang on to the ragged edge of consciousness—mainly out of fear, I'll admit. I wasn't sure I'd wake up again.

I weigh about 220. They couldn't just carry me and the stretcher. They had to let the front end roll where it could, lifting it only when they had no choice. The downhill end, though, had to be lifted pretty much all the time. Pete took that end. He was a husky man, nearly as big as me, but that slope defeated him. After a few nearly vertical yards he tripped or slipped and set his end down suddenly. And hard.

I heard myself cry out. It took everything I had to fight off the black, greasy wave. Then I heard *her* voice. She was arguing with them.

She won the argument. While I was busy breathing, she took over at the head of the stretcher, leaving the downhill end to the two men. Not that I figured this out at the time. Then, I was only aware of pain. The need to stay conscious. And that she was near enough to touch me again, because she did.

"Stubborn man," she whispered. Her hand was warm on my cheek, so warm. Almost hot. That heat seemed to push me right out of myself. I lost my grip on consciousness and tumbled off into the darkness.

Two

I knew where I was before I opened my eyes. The emergency room at Fleetwood Memorial Hospital was a place of bad smells, beeping monitors and people who wouldn't listen to me.

"Deep puncture wound in the clavicular portion of the right pectoralis major," someone was saying rapidly. "Some involvement of the deltoid. Patient complained of head pain earlier."

"He was conscious? Responsive?"

"At the scene, yes. He passed out when we carried him to the ambulance. After administering Ringer's…BP holding steady. Pulse…"

The voices were fading in and out. My head ached and my shoulder was one huge, monstrous throb, but I didn't feel as sick and dizzy as I had before. Weak, though. And tired. It was hard to pay attention, tempting to let myself drift off again. But if I did, other people would be making the decisions for me. I didn't like that.

"You didn't use a neck brace." That was a prissy male voice. "The neck is to be supported in all vehicular accidents."

"He crawled more than fifty yards up a mountain," Pete retorted. "I don't think his neck is broken."

"Come on—get him on the table."

That meant they were going to move me again. I blinked gummy lids and was immediately blinded by the overhead light. "Where…" The oxygen mask muffled my voice. I turned my head and tried to dislodge it.

"Mr. McClain." A man's face hovered over mine briefly, haloed by the too-bright light. I couldn't make out his features. "I'm Dr. Meckle. You've been in an accident, and you're at the emergency room."

Well, dammit, I knew that. "Get this off me," I said, but even to me the words were unintelligible.

"You must be still. We're going to move you now."

They did. I had to pay attention to my breathing again. While I was working on that, the prissy doctor was tossing out orders like General Sherman reviewing the troops. "Get his clothes cut off. Draw some blood and get it typed and cross-matched. Aguilar, is this the only wound you found?"

"Yes, sir."

"Doesn't add up," he muttered. "This dressing is almost clean."

Someone jabbed my good arm with a needle and I realized that it wasn't strapped down anymore. Good. As soon as she pulled the needle out, I reached up and shoved the oxygen mask down. "Where is she? The woman. Paramedic."

"The paramedics who brought you in are both men," the doctor said. There was something irritating about his voice. And familiar. "Now, sir, please cooperate. You've lost a good deal of blood. You aren't thinking clearly."

Pete spoke up. "I think he's talking about the woman who found him. The officer at the scene was going to send her here. Exposure or something like that."

"What? What's wrong with her?" I needed to sit up.

"Aguilar," the doctor snapped, planting a hand firmly on my good shoulder, "if you're determined to clutter up my examination room, at least do so silently. Mr. McClain, I will promise to check on this mystery woman once I'm satisfied with your condition. Be *still*."

I subsided, unable to do much else. What had happened to her? Exposure…had she put her coat over me, and suffered for it? I couldn't remember. The officer at the scene…oh, God. Duncan. Duncan worked nights. He would hear about my accident on the police radio, and think I was dead or something. "I need—"

"What you need, Mr. McClain, is medical attention. Which I am attempting to give you. If you won't hold still, I will have you strapped down. Roberts, get that mask back on him."

The world was taking on that sick spin again, which was the fault of that prissy doctor. I wouldn't be so wiped out if he'd quit arguing and cooperate. As it was, the nurse defeated me easily, fitting the mask over my face. I decided to suck down some of the oxygen they were determined to give me, get my strength back and try again.

"Not enough blood," he muttered as he snipped at whatever was holding my shoulder together. "The man's in shock, there should be…what the hell?"

I didn't like the sound of that.

"What is it?" one of the medical crowd asked.

"Look at this. There, see?" He pointed at my shoulder, not quite touching it. I couldn't see a thing. His hands were in the way. "That's newly formed flesh. And this section is scabbed over. That's not right. It's…" He looked at me accusingly. "Mr. McClain. This is an old injury, isn't it? Several days old, at least."

Idiot. I stared at him stonily over the top of the oxygen mask.

He sighed and pulled the mask down. "Did you injure your shoulder a few days ago?"

"No. I think a tree limb punched through the window and pierced it when my truck rolled. I—"

"Impossible."

Obviously not, since it had happened. But arguing with idiots is a waste of breath, and I didn't have breath to spare. "I need to call my brother—Officer Duncan McClain."

"You did not lose any substantial amount of blood from this wound tonight."

I gave up and turned my head. "Pete, I need to call Duncan."

Pete looked at me helplessly. "I imagine someone has already called him. He'll be here soon."

"No!" I'd had enough of lying flat while everyone ignored me. I struggled up onto one elbow. Things spun for a second and my forehead turned clammy, but I made it.

"Lie *down,* Mr. McClain."

"Why? You decided maybe I am hurt, after all? Pete, I need to call Duncan myself. Don't want him worried. I—"

"This man creating a disturbance?" said a voice from the doorway.

"I tried to stop him, Doctor," said a harried female. "He wouldn't listen."

Relief hit like a slap in the face, puncturing my anger. My strength drained right out with it, so I let the nurse ease me back down. "I'm okay, Duncan."

"Yeah?" The man who cut through the medical crowd to stand by my bed was shorter and lighter than I am. Better looking, too, with smoother features and eyes as pale as mine are dark. We have the same hair, though. Dark brown and board straight.

Duncan had on his blank face, the one that makes him a good cop and annoys the hell out of me. Never have been able to read the boy when he doesn't want to be read. He put a hand on my good shoulder and squeezed lightly. "I can see that you are."

"I am," I insisted. But I was sure tired, and the pain wasn't coming in waves anymore. It was this huge, steady presence, almost solid. I felt as if I'd bounced myself off that solid mass of pain a few times too many and rattled my brains. "Truck's a mess, though."

One side of Duncan's mouth quirked up. "You've looked better yourself."

"Yeah, well...I tried to call you, but this stupid—"

"Now, now," he said.

"Belligerence is not uncommon with those in shock," the doctor said, all pompous and tolerant. "I'm afraid your brother's attitude is impeding his treatment, however. Normally I would not allow a family member to be present at this point, but if you can persuade him to cooperate, Officer, you may remain."

As if he could *stop* Duncan. I snorted.

"Belligerent, is he?" For some reason that made Duncan smile. He squeezed my good shoulder again. Anxiety nestled in the corners of his eyes, keeping the smile out, but I could read him now.

I relaxed. If Duncan didn't need his blank face, he wasn't too upset.

"You heard the man, Ben. Play nice."

"Man's an idiot," I muttered, but someone had tied weights on my eyelids. They were closing in spite of me. It was all right, though. Duncan would keep an eye on the idiot. He'd take care of things. "You'll tell Zach…make it so he doesn't worry."

"I will."

Good. That was good. The darkness beckoned, no longer threatening. "And the angel," I murmured as I let myself go. "You'll find her for me."

Doctors and nurses are not reasonable people.

No question about who was in charge, and it wasn't me. Admittedly, I wasn't in any shape to go home right away. After they'd finished poking and stitching and X-raying me, pumping me full of antibiotics and O-negative, they finally strapped me into a fancy sling and put me in a room where I could get some sleep. Then, of course, they kept waking me up.

In spite of this, I felt a lot better by late afternoon. But no one was interested in my opinion of my condition. Mostly they seemed irritated that it wasn't worse. At least that prissy E.R. doctor was out of the picture now.

I'd finally remembered where I knew him from. Twenty-some years ago, Harold Meckle, M.D., had been a couple of grades behind me in school. Harry had been a certified brain back then, so he was probably a competent doctor now. But it would take a personality transplant to turn him into a competent human being.

Harry had a real bee in his bonnet about my shoulder. At one point he'd actually wanted to do surgery in order to find out why I didn't need surgery. He was convinced I had to have some internal injury that was bleeding like a mother to account for all the blood I'd lost.

Fortunately, my own doctor had arrived by then. Dr. Miller didn't see any point in cutting me open to satisfy Harry's curiosity. Or, as he put it, he preferred a conservative approach, which meant keeping me under observation. Which meant keeping me in the hospital.

I'm a reasonable man. I could see that they needed to hold on to me awhile. I had a concussion, among other things. That's why they'd woken me up every blasted hour on the hour, until I finally stayed awake in self-defense.

I knew all that. I just didn't like it.

Shortly before supper a skinny little blonde showed up carrying a plastic sack from a department store. Her pink sweater was big enough for two of her, hiding what I knew to be a curvy bottom. She'd cut her hair again, I noticed. For some reason she liked it short. Long or short, I enjoyed looking at her hair. It was a pale, shiny blond, like sunshine on freshly cut pine.

Her name was Gwen. She was my son's mother and—as of three months ago—my brother's wife.

"I've got a book on Samuel Adams I hope you haven't read," she said, bustling up to my bed, where she deposited a peck on my cheek and the sack on my bed. "Also two magazines, a crossword puzzle book and some pajamas so you don't have to wear that hospital gown. You're looking better, I must say, though your bruises are coming out nicely. How are you feeling?"

"Hungry. Where's Duncan? With Zach?" I used my good arm to dig through the sack. The pajamas were new, of course, since I didn't own any. I wondered how much of a fuss she'd make when I paid her back for them.

"Duncan is getting something else I understand you asked for. Zach is with Mrs. Bradshaw."

"How's he taking all this? He's not too upset?"

She smiled. "We may have overdone the reassuring. He wanted to know if you'd still take him camping this weekend."

"We" meant her and Duncan. I was getting used to that. I grimaced. "We're likely to have had our first snow by the time all the dings in my carcass have healed enough for me to take him."

"Probably. He'll survive waiting until next spring. Oh, I talked to Edie. She wants you to let her know if there's anything she can do."

She might try leaving me alone. One date is not a lifetime commitment. Couldn't say that, though. The woman was a friend of Gwen's. "What about Annie? Did Duncan ever get hold of her?" I knew Duncan had called Charlie, my youngest brother, but Annie was harder to get hold of.

My little sister was currently in a tiny village in Guatemala with her husband, Jack, a construction engineer who works for a nonprofit organization. ICA builds schools and hospitals and such in developing countries. Right now, Jack was putting up a clinic while Annie taught the kids in a one-room, dirt-floor hut.

I still hadn't gotten used to her being so far away most of the time.

"Oh, yes. Sorry—I forgot to mention that. I talked to her after lunch. She's worried, naturally, but I persuaded her to hold off on buying a plane ticket."

I would have liked to see her…but that was selfish. She was needed where she was. I pulled out the book Gwen had brought. "I've been wanting to read this one. Thanks. But you forgot something."

"No, I didn't."

"My clothes."

"If I bring you clothes, you'll put them on. Duncan spoke to your doctor, Ben, so don't think you can put one over on us. You are staying here at least two more days."

I was patient with her. "I'm not planning to leave the hospital without Dr. Miller's okay. He's a sensible man, unlike the idiot in the E.R. I just want to have the *option* of leaving."

"You get the clothes when Dr. Miller releases you, and not a minute before."

"Dammit, Gwen, I'm not a two-year-old!"

"You're as stubborn as one! You've got a concussion, a banged-up knee, a big hole in your shoulder and a broken clavicle. You're not going anywhere right away, and when they do discharge you, you'll be coming home with me and Duncan."

No way in hell was that going to happen. "You live on the second floor. I'm not up to handling stairs yet."

"You're not discharged yet, either." She fussed with the flowers and stuff on the table by my bed, making room for the things she'd brought. "And once you are, you can lie around on the couch like a sultan and order everyone around. That should suit you."

Gwen had adapted well to being my sister-in-law. She sounded more like my sister all the time. Snippy. "I thought I was too banged up for Zach to see. That's why you didn't want to sneak him in here." That, and the fact that, being an attorney, Gwen has a thing about rules, and the hospital didn't allow kids under ten to visit.

"I'm sure you'll look better by the time you're released." She quit messing with the flowers and faced me. "You are not going home to an empty house in your condition, Ben. Forget that idea."

That hit too close to home. When I heard the snick of the door opening I turned to face it, relieved. Someone probably wanted more of my blood, or to see how "we" were doing, but that was okay. Better than looking at the concern in Gwen's eyes.

"You up for some visitors?" Duncan asked.

Even better. I smiled. "You're not a visitor, you're a…" My voice trailed off. I forgot what I was going to say.

He'd found her. Duncan had found my angel.

Only she wasn't, of course. Not mine, and certainly not an angel. A Valkyrie, maybe. Or an amazon. The top of her head was level with my brother's, and Duncan hits a fraction over six feet.

Her sweatshirt was blue and sloppy beneath a worn yellow parka, but couldn't disguise beautiful, half-moon breasts. Faded denim stretched tight over a couple miles of legs—firm, rounded, muscular legs. Her hair was a messy riot of brown curls tumbling well below her shoulders. She was built long and lush, strong and stacked, every inch of her pure woman.

It was a body that made quite an impact on a man. I blinked a few times before I got my gaze back to her face. That looked the same as I remembered…except, of course, she wasn't glowing.

"I don't think you two were ever introduced," Duncan said. "Ben, this is Seely Jones. Seely, this is my brother Ben—Benjamin McClain—and my wife, Gwen."

I had no idea what to say. I hadn't thought beyond finding her, seeing her again. I cleared my throat. "Unusual name."

"My mother is an unusual woman." She turned her smile on Gwen. "You have a very persistent husband. Nice, but persistent."

Gwen and Duncan exchanged one of those private smiles. "Yes, I do. I hope his persistence hasn't inconvenienced you too much. I'm very glad to meet you."

"You're okay, aren't you?" I said. "I heard you were treated and released, but no one would tell me what you'd been treated for."

"Oh, that. I'm afraid I scared the police officer who was taking my statement by fainting, so they felt obliged to bring me in."

I'd never seen a woman who looked less likely to faint in my life.

My expression must have given my thoughts away, for she laughed. "Absurd, isn't it? I've done it all my life, though. Not often, thank goodness, and no, it is not a symptom of some dreadful underlying health problem—though I did have some trouble persuading the E.R. doctor of that. You seem to be doing well."

"Thanks to you. I, uh…that's what I wanted. To thank you."

She smiled that slow, sweet smile I remembered. "Daisy says everything happens for a reason, but I never thought I'd be grateful to Vic."

"Vic?" I frowned. "You don't mean Victor Sorenson."

"Don't I?" Her eyebrows went up in elaborate surprise. "I thought I did." She ambled up to my bed, *click-click-click.*

I glanced down. She was wearing high heels. My own eyebrows went up. Got to respect the moxie of a tall woman who chooses to wear three-inch heels. "Sorenson's a worm," I mentioned, in case she hadn't noticed.

"I'll agree with you there." She spoke the way she moved—slow and easy, as if she'd never hurried in her life and didn't intend to start. "He fired me last night. That's why I left the resort so late and ended up finding you. Which is a roundabout sort of gratitude, but there you go. Roundabout is probably the only kind of appreciation Vic's likely to get."

"I didn't know Vic kept a paramedic on staff."

"I was working as a waitress, not a paramedic." Her voice didn't change but her eyes did—as if she'd closed a door, gently but firmly, on that subject. "Vic and I disagreed about the fringe benefits of the job. He thought he was one of them. I didn't."

The thought of Vic putting his hands on this woman made me furious. "I'll talk to him," I promised grimly.

Duncan gave me a level look. "Don't do anything I'd have to arrest you for."

"You should consider filing suit against him," Gwen said seriously. "Sexual harassment is wrong, and firing you for failing to agree to his demands—well, it sounds like you'd have a good case."

"Oh, he didn't fire me because I wouldn't go to bed with him. I think it was the cannelloni," Seely said thoughtfully. "It didn't go with his suit. Or maybe it was the chicken-fried steak. There was all that cream gravy, you see. He was not happy about the gravy."

A laugh took me by surprise. It hurt, so I stopped. "Dumped a tray on him, did you?"

Her mouth stayed solemn, but her eyes laughed along with me. Extraordinary eyes. Not the color—they were blue, pretty enough, but nothing unusual. Maybe it was their shape, sort of elongated, with a flirty tilt at the corners. Or the way they seemed to offer confidences, as if she and I were old friends who didn't need to put everything into words.

"I found Miss Jones at the bus station," Duncan said. "She was buying a ticket to Denver."

A frown snapped down. "You're leaving town?"

"Why not? I lost my job."

"But you have a car. What were you doing at the bus station?"

She pulled a face. "The stupid thing decided to die on me. The mechanic says it's either some gasket or the whole motor, and he can't say which without taking everything apart, which will cost a fortune. You'd think he could tell the difference, wouldn't you?"

"Head gasket, sounds like," I said, my brain clicking away on an idea. "Or the heads themselves. You must have lost compression."

"You do speak the lingo," she said admiringly.

Duncan asked her who she'd taken the car to, then assured her that Ron was a good mechanic. Gwen was looking fidgety.

"But your things!" she burst out. "I can understand leaving your car if it wasn't worth repairing, but surely you couldn't take everything with you on the bus. Even if you didn't have furniture, there's clothes, dishes, bedding…oh." An embarrassed flush sped over her cheeks. "It isn't any of my business, is it?"

Seely turned that lazy smile Gwen's way. "Probably not, but we can't help being curious about people, can we? I don't have much stuff, being more of a wanderer than a nester. No dishes or bedding. A few keepsakes and some clothes, yes, but not that many. Susan seemed happy to accept what I didn't want to take with me."

"Susan?" I said, only half my brain on what she was saying.

"Another waitress at the resort. I'd been rooming with her, but I don't think she minded my sudden departure. She's had her eye on Vic for a while. Well." She shrugged, a graceful movement that did lovely things to her breasts. "No accounting for tastes, is there?"

Things were falling into place. "You decided to leave more or less on impulse, then?"

"I do a lot of things on impulse."

"Then there's nothing waiting for you in Denver? No reason you need to be there right away?"

She used her eyebrows to ask where I was going with all this.

"My brother and sister-in-law think I'm going to need some help after I leave the hospital tomorrow."

Gwen interrupted. "*Not* tomorrow, Ben."

"They can't do anything more for me here. Besides, hospitals are unhealthy. People get staph infections in hospitals. Now, Gwen and Duncan might be right about me needing a little help—"

Duncan snorted.

"So I was thinking maybe you'd be interested. You need a job, right? And a place to stay while your car gets fixed."

"I..." For the first time, her composure was shaken. "Weren't you listening? I wasn't planning to fix my car."

I brushed that aside. "Look, if you're worried about staying with a man you don't know, I'm not in any shape to give you a hard time." Gwen muttered something about my being able to give people a hard time on my deathbed. I ignored that. "Not that I would hassle you, anyway, but you couldn't know that."

She shook her head. "That's not it."

"What's the problem, then?" I used my left elbow to prop myself up.

Everything went gray. The next thing I knew, Seely was depositing me efficiently back on my pillows. I'm not sure how she got there before Duncan, who isn't exactly slow off the mark, but she did.

"There's a line between stubborn and stupid," she said, looking down at me. "Something tells me you cross it now and then."

Duncan grinned. Gwen giggled. I scowled. "I moved too fast, that's all."

"Uh-huh," Seely said. "I can see you'll undo everyone's work, given half a chance. All right. I'll take the job."

Hot damn. "Good. That's good."

"On two conditions. First, you stay in the hospital until the doctor releases you. Second, you'll do as I tell you while you're under my care."

"Now, wait a minute—"

"He agrees," Duncan said firmly. "Don't you, Ben?"

Seely's lips twitched, but she looked at me steadily, waiting. With a sigh, I nodded. "Within reason."

Gwen spoke. "I hate to put a stick in the spokes, but you really should tell her about Doofus."

Seely did that question-thing with her eyebrows. "Zach's dog," I explained. "My son. He lives with me. Doofus, I mean." Relief had hit, followed by a wave of exhaustion. It was hard to get words lined up right. "Zach's in kindergarten. He comes over after school some days."

"My point is that Doofus is a puppy, not a dog," Gwen said. "You should be aware you're not just taking on one large, slightly snarly man. The man is at least housetrained. Doofus isn't."

"Thanks a lot, Gwen."

Seely's lips tipped up. "I think I can handle a puppy, as long as Ben can handle being bossed around."

"Within reason," I repeated. When she nodded, I breathed a sigh of relief. "All right, then. We've got a deal."

Duncan was amused, Gwen was relieved, and Seely...I couldn't tell. Her cheeks were flushed, her mouth smiling, but her eyes seemed distracted, like she was taking a serious look inward.

And me? I was satisfied...for now. "Don't you want to know how much the job will pay?"

"Money's not a big issue for me."

"Uh—you aren't rich or something, are you?"

Gwen made a choked sound that she turned into clearing

her throat. Seely laughed and tucked her hair back from her face. "I've been accused of a number of oddities, but rich isn't one of them."

The movement drew my attention to the long dangles of multicolored glass hanging from her ears. They reminded me…I glanced at her wrist.

Yes. That was the bracelet I remembered. "Pretty bracelet."

Her eyebrows lifted gently. "Thanks. The stones represent the chakras. I'm guessing by the look on your face that you know what chakras are?"

"I read." Bunch of New Age nonsense, but I wouldn't say that to the woman who'd saved my life.

Everyone wanted me to rest then. I was willing to let them have their way as soon as I'd passed on some instructions for Manny, who was going to have to run things at McClain Construction for awhile. They were right—I was tired.

And I'd gotten what I wanted.

I'd stay here one more night, then I was going home. Not to an empty house, either. Seely would be there. I didn't think Dr. Miller would give me grief over leaving the hospital once he knew I'd have trained medical help around. And I wouldn't have to come up with any more reasons not to stay with Duncan while I was recovering.

Don't get me wrong. I love my brother. Unfortunately, I also love his wife.

Three

Outside, the birds were making a fuss about morning. It was a familiar sound, even this late in the year. There were always a few who wintered over. But usually I didn't listen to their chatter from a hospital bed in the den.

I sat on the edge of that bed and glared at my knee.

I had no idea how it had gotten hurt, no memory of it bothering me during my crawl up the mountain, but it was swollen to twice its size. Soft-tissue damage, according to the doctor. The swelling should go down in a few days. I was to stay off it as much as possible.

The downstairs bathroom was two rooms and half a hallway away.

All the bedrooms in the house were on the second floor, which is why they'd parked me in the den when I came home yesterday. The den was an addition, tacked on at the very back of the house. The bathroom was opposite the laundry room.

I'd put up with using a plastic basin to brush my teeth, but I was damned if I was going to pee in the stupid urinal they'd sent me home with.

Besides, I wanted more coffee. And something to *do*. There was a TV in here, but I wasn't much for television. I like to read, but not all day. The table by my bed held sickroom paraphernalia—water, a glass, pain pills, the stuff Gwen had brought me in the hospital. My laptop, though I'd practically had to sign an oath in blood that I wouldn't use it to work yet. A little bell I was supposed to ring if I needed anything.

I grimaced at that bell. Last night I'd barely managed one game of solitaire on my laptop. Seely had come in to refill my water and see how I was doing. I'd fallen asleep so fast I wasn't sure I'd answered her.

I'd done nothing but sleep yesterday. I was sick of it.

On the floor next to the bed, Doofus was growling. He'd sunk his sharp little baby teeth into a dangling corner of my blanket and was killing it. In the kitchen, the radio was playing softly. I could hear quiet, moving-around noises, too…water running at the sink. The refrigerator door opening and closing.

That would be Seely, clearing up after breakfast. She'd brought me eggs and toast in bed.

Damned if I know why people consider breakfast in bed a treat. Even with a bed you can crank to a sitting position, it's a pain. Besides, I'd had enough of beds. I wanted to shave. I wanted a shower and real clothes, not wrinkled pajamas. I needed to talk to Manny, and my loving family had persuaded Seely not to leave the phone by my bed.

First things first. I stood slowly, having learned that I got dizzy if I tried to move too fast. It was nice, I decided, to hear a woman puttering around in the kitchen. I wondered how much of a squawk Seely would make when I joined her there. A grin tugged at my mouth.

Funny. I was in a pretty good mood, considering I'd smashed my truck and put some major dents in several body parts. But it was good to be home…good to have survived to come home.

I started across the room. Contrary to my family's fondly held opinion, I know my limits. I'd lost a lot of blood, which meant I was going to be weak, sometimes dizzy. Combine that with a knee not inclined to take much weight, a shoulder that kept me from using crutches and a body that was stiff and sore everywhere but my left big toe, and falling was a real possibility. Especially with that fool puppy running circles around my feet.

I took it slow and careful. I wanted to make a point. I also wanted coffee and conversation, maybe some answers. I limped into the dining room, frowning.

In any contest between memory and logic, logic ought to win. Women don't glow. I knew that. I'd been in bad shape when Seely found me, my perceptions skewed by a system on the verge of shutting down. I couldn't trust my memory.

Yet that one memory bead remained so clear…the curves of her face as she smiled at me, the tilt of her eyes, the way her breath had puffed out, ghostly in the cold air. And the gentle luminescence of her skin, like moonlight on snow. Not at all like a flashlight. Just as clearly I remember the warmth, a heat that had sunk itself into me instead of sitting around on the surface.

I had questions, and I couldn't let them go.

I managed to avoid tripping over Doofus as I left the bathroom, but had to pause in the doorway to the kitchen, one hand on the jamb to steady myself. The sling supported my shoulder, so it wasn't hurting too much. Unlike my knee.

Seely was wiping down the counter, humming along with the radio. She wore jeans and a blue sweater today, and her denim-clad hips were swaying to the music in a cute little be-bop that yanked my attention away from my sore knee.

Then I noticed what was playing on the radio: Kenny Chesney singing "How forever feels." The song Gwen and I had danced to five years ago, on the night we'd ended up in bed together.

The night before I left her.

All the fizz drained out of the day. I took a deep breath and limped on into the room. Doofus yelped happily, announcing our arrival.

Seely spun around, her eyes wide. "How do you do that?"

"What?" Doofus had found his water dish and was thrilled by the discovery, lapping away as if he'd been in the desert for days. I'd have to put him out soon. Or ask Seely to, dammit. I didn't like depending on others for every little thing.

"Sneak up on me when you can barely walk," she said.

"No shoes." I decided to rest a bit before making for the oak table in the center of the room. "I came out for a cup of coffee."

"I would have brought you coffee. That's what that little bell by your bed is for."

"I didn't want to drink it in bed. Besides, I thought it would help if you could see that I'm able to move around some now."

"Help what?"

"I don't want to sleep all day today."

One of her eyebrows lifted. The woman had the most talkative eyebrows I'd ever seen. "Okay. You thought I needed to be notified of this?"

Yesterday I'd dozed off every time she checked on me. That had to be coincidence…didn't it? "We have a deal. I do what you say, within reason. I wanted to show you that it wouldn't be reasonable to keep me in bed all day."

Her mouth kicked up on one side. "Well, since you're already here, you may as well sit down and have that coffee. No, wait—I'd rather you didn't go splat on the floor. Let me get on your good side first."

I didn't have much choice. She reached me before I'd taken more than a couple of halting steps and slid an arm around my waist. The warm strength of her body felt good. "How can you move so fast without seeming to hurry?"

"Long legs. It helps when my target is crippled and can' escape."

My mouth twitched. The top of her head was only a few inches below mine. If I'd turned my head, it would have tickled my nose. Her hair smelled nice—a green smell, like herbs.

We made for the table at a half lurch, and I had to admit it was easier with her help. More pleasant, too. My body started entertaining ideas I could have sworn it wasn't ready to consider yet. I sure couldn't do anything about those ideas, even if I'd been free to.

Which I wasn't. She was an employee, off-limits.

We reached the table. I spoke abruptly. "The first time I saw you, you were glowing."

"Amazing the sort of thing a mind in shock can conjure, isn't it?"

"Is that what it was?"

She let me go as I lowered myself carefully into a chair, then looked me square in the eye. Her eyebrows were expressing skepticism. "I don't know. Do you often see people glow when you aren't in shock?"

"Hardly ever." Common wisdom holds that people won't look you in the eye if they're lying. This is stupid. Since everyone knows this, someone who intends to lie to you will be sure to meet your eyes. I guess people who expect liars to look shifty haven't been around teenagers much. "That E.R. doctor was sure baffled by my shoulder."

She laughed and headed for the coffeepot. "The one you kept calling an idiot?"

"Yeah. Harry Meckle. I knew him in school." Was she dodging the subject? Or was I being given a chance to avoid looking like a fool? I drummed my fingers on the table. "I want you to tell Gwen it's okay for Zach to come over after school today."

"Uh-uh." She set a steaming mug in front of me. The multicolored stones in her bracelet glittered.

"Do you wear that all the time?"

"Hmm? Oh." She sat down, keeping another mug for herself. "The bracelet. Yes, pretty much."

"So why won't you talk to Gwen for me?"

"I never step between dueling exes."

"Gwen and I aren't dueling. We aren't even exes. We were never married." I held myself ready for the questions that were sure to come. People were invariably nosy about me, Gwen, Zach and Duncan.

Seely shrugged. "So? You're obviously ex-somethings."

I'd never thought of it that way. For some reason the notion settled me, as if some little wandering piece had finally found its spot. I took a sip of coffee. "This is good."

"Thanks."

"The thing is, Zach has had enough uncertainty in his life. I think it will be good for him to see that, yeah, I'm banged up but I'm basically okay."

"I won't argue with that, but can't you just tell Gwen yourself?"

I grimaced. "My family has some funny ideas. They think I don't know my own limitations."

She sipped her coffee, her eyes laughing at me over the rim. "Maybe you've given them some teensie-weensie reason to think that?"

"No." I was certain about that. "Couldn't have. I've never been really hurt before. A few stitches here and there, yeah, but nothing they kept me for overnight. Never been in any kind of auto accident."

"Never? Not even a fender-bender?"

I shook my head and thought sadly about my truck.

"I imagine you scared them, then. They probably don't realize it, but deep down I'll bet they think you're invulnerable."

"They're annoying sometimes, but they aren't stupid."

"Feelings don't always follow logic, do they? They probably needed you to be invulnerable when they were younger. You were all they had."

I scowled. "Who told you that?"

"Oh, it came up in different ways. While you were napping yesterday, you had visitors. Manny Holstedder—I gather he works for you?—and two of your neighbors, and of course Duncan. And phone calls. I made a list you can look at later, but I do recall that your sister Annie called, and another brother. Charlie, I think? And Edie Snelling called twice." She put just enough lift at the end of that to make it almost a question.

"A friend of Gwen's," I muttered. There are worse things than an ex-lover who's determined to fix you up. Falling off a mountain, for example. But dammit, I wished Gwen would quit trying to slide women under my door.

"Mmm. Anyway, your friends, family and neighbors all wanted me to know I was taking care of someone special. You're something of a hero, you know."

"Oh, for God's sake—"

"No, really. They all think you're pretty grand. Several of them told me about the way you took over raising your sister and brothers after your folks were killed."

Mortified, I nearly burned my tongue on the coffee. I set the mug down and cleared my throat. "To get back to the subject—I thought you could assure Gwen that I'm up to having Zach come over. That is…I never asked. Are you okay with having a five-year-old around?"

"Sure. I like kids."

"I guess you don't have any of your own. You said you weren't a nester."

She tipped her head to one side. Her curls were semitamed today, caught back in a stretchy blue thing at her nape. A few strands had wiggled free. "Are you really curious, or just paying me back for having learned so much about you when you were helpless?"

That surprised a chuckle out of me.

Oddly, she shivered. It was a delicate little thing, but I caught it. "Are you cold? We can turn up the heat."

"No," she said absently, rubbing her left palm as if it itched. "You do have a deep voice, don't you? It sounds as if it's rolling up from the bottom of a well. Oh, look—Doofus is actually at the door, asking to go out. I'd better reward that."

She liked the sound of my voice. That's what that little shiver had meant. I enjoyed that notion about as much as I did watching her as she ambled for the back door. The way those long legs carried her along put a nice little sway in her hips. Those legs…

She opened the back door and Doofus scampered out. "How did you pick Doofus?"

"The name or the dog?"

"Both, I guess. A bit of unique, isn't he?"

"That's one way to put it. No, leave the door open. He panics if you close it, then forgets what he went outside to do." A man could die happy with those legs wrapped around him—whoa. A little sexual buzz was okay, but I couldn't let myself get carried away. "I got him from the pound for Zach's fifth birthday. The vet says he's a basset mix, emphasis on the mix."

She glanced out the door. "The ears do look have the look of a basset hound. Zach comes over to play with him fairly often, I take it?"

"Two or three days a week. A neighbor's teenage daughter walks him here from the school when the weather is decent. Sometimes to Mrs. Bradshaw's, if I can't be home at that hour."

"That's your neighbor, right? She stopped by yesterday to see how you were doing."

"She keeps kids." That still didn't sit too well with me. I didn't want Zach raised by anyone other than family. But Mrs. Bradshaw was a good woman, and he liked it there. As Gwen often pointed out, at Mrs. Bradshaw's he had other kids to play with, most notably a set of twins. "You never did answer my question."

"Your…oh. About children." Doofus scampered back in, the whole back half of his body wagging with delight over his performance. She shut the door and knelt to praise and pat. "Nope, no kids of my own. No stepchildren, nieces or nephews, either. I've never been married, and I was an only child."

So was Gwen. Putting the two women together in my mind made me uncomfortable. I shifted, stretching out my bad leg. "I guess that would be lonely, being an only child."

"I had my fantasies about having a brother or sister when I was growing up. But a lot of people from big families fantasize about being an only, I think. Didn't you?"

"No more than four or five times a day. Especially when Charlie and Annie were teenagers. Not that Annie got into any real trouble, but she was a girl. There's so much *stuff* about being a girl at that age…" I shook my head. "I wanted to lock her up or send her to a convent. Raising girls is scary."

"She's quite a bit younger than you, I gather."

"Eleven years, yeah. She's the youngest." I hadn't done right by Annie. For years she'd had a kind of phobia about leaving Highpoint, and I hadn't even realized it—probably because I'd liked having her around too much to question why she'd moved back home and stayed. Jack had known, though. He'd married her and taken her off to see the world, one dirt-poor village at a time. And she loved it. I frowned at my coffee cup.

"More coffee?"

I shook my head. "No, thanks. Ah…jeans probably won't work with this stupid knee. There ought to be a pair of sweats in the bottom left drawer of my dresser, though. If you'd get them, I can have my shower in the downstairs bathroom, then get dressed."

"You are not—" she started, then stopped, shaking her head. "Who'd have thought you'd be so devious?"

I scowled. "What are you talking about?"

"I'm supposed to fuss at you, remind you of what the doctor said, et cetera. In the end, you'll give up on the shower, and I'm supposed to concede that you can get dressed. Which is what you really want."

"Are you sure you don't have brothers?"

She chuckled. "Nary a one."

Yet she obviously knew men. Well, she'd probably had plenty of opportunity to observe my half of the species. That showgirl's body would get any man's attention. Then he'd get hooked by that slow smile, or the way her eyes crinkled at the corners, laughing all by themselves. "You aren't giving me a hard time about getting dressed," I observed.

"Not much point. I knew you'd be champing at the bit today. You do realize I'll have to help you, don't you?"

"Like hell you will."

She just looked at me. For once, even her eyebrows didn't comment.

At last I sighed. "The shirt. I'll need help with that. And the sling."

"I could give you a sponge bath first."

A visceral flash hit me—her hands running a warm, soapy washcloth along my arm to my shoulder, then down my chest...she'd be bending over me, bringing those magnificent breasts close enough to... "No, you can't."

Like I said, I know my limits.

Four

I couldn't reach my left foot. I glared at my knee, washcloth in hand.

I was sitting on the toilet with the lid down. I'd managed a spit bath of sorts, pulled on my shorts and sweatpants…and one sock. I couldn't get my left sock on. And I couldn't wash my own damned foot.

Everything throbbed—head, shoulder, knee. My feet were cold. I was going to have to ask for help.

Someone knocked on the bathroom door.

"Yeah?" I growled.

"Thought you might be ready for a cup of coffee," Seely said through the door. "And an extra hand. As I recall, I had the devil of a time with shoes and socks when my wrist was broken."

I sighed. "It's unlocked. How did you break your wrist?"

The door swung open. "I wasn't a very coordinated child.

Fell from the monkey bars when I was seven. Daisy had to do everything for me at first, which sorely offended my dignity. Here." She held out a tall walking stick. "Duncan dug this up in the attic yesterday. He thought you might be able to use it."

I put down the washcloth and took the stick. It was made of walnut, a dark, burled wood that felt smooth and cool to my fingers. "How about that." I smiled, bemused. "I'd forgotten all about this thing. Funny. I must have seen my father use it a hundred times, but the one time that floated into my head just now…"

"Yes?" She set the mug on the tiny bit of counter next to the sink.

"We were in Crete. Me and my dad, that is. Annie was only a month old, so my mom wasn't able to go with my dad that year." I leaned the stick against the wall. There wasn't really room for it in this little scrap of a bathroom, but it made me feel good to have it near. "We'd climbed this little rise overlooking the dig, and he was using his stick to point out a city that didn't exist anymore. All I saw was this reddish maze of crumbling walls in the section that had been excavated. He saw so much more—the granary, the wide, dusty street leading to the temple. Maybe even the people on that street."

"He had vision. It sounds like a good memory."

"Yeah." I thought about how excited I'd been to go with him. How hard I'd tried to see what he did…and failed. "It was the first time I'd gone with him. I guess that's why that memory sticks out."

"How old were you?"

"Eleven. It was summer, of course. I remember—hey!"

She'd knelt and was reaching for my foot. "Must have been hot."

"Blazing. You don't have to do that." I tried to retrieve my foot without creating a tug-of-war.

"Quit that or I'll tickle you." She ran the washcloth over my sole. "I'll admit I'm not a real nurse, but I'm pretty sure this sort of thing is part of the job."

I scowled. This was every bit as embarrassing as I'd thought it would be. "No, you're a paramedic. So why aren't you working as one?"

"Because I couldn't hack it." She grabbed the towel. "So why is your brother married to your son's mother instead of you?"

Sucker-punched. I hadn't seen that one coming, and for a second couldn't think of a thing to say.

"I'm sorry. I shouldn't have said that." She dried my foot carefully, giving me the top of her head to look at instead of her face. Even with her hair pulled back, her hair was all crinkly, like a shallow stream wiggling over rocks.

Or like Doofus wiggling all over even when he was trying to stand still. I sighed. I felt as if I'd just kicked a puppy— and gotten bitten for it. "Don't apologize. I asked for it. I jabbed at you because I don't like needing help for every little thing. Can't complain if you jab back."

"Okay. Hand me your socks, will you?"

I did, and she pulled a sock on my left foot. It felt weird to sit there while she did that. "I'm surprised none of the busybodies you talked to yesterday filled you in about me and Gwen."

Seely looked up then, her face all smoothed out. "I really am sorry. I'm not usually such a bitch."

That annoyed me. "You're not a bitch at all."

"I can be, when my temper's up."

"I have a temper, too, but no one calls me a bitch."

She laughed. "I have a feeling no one calls you anything but 'sir' when you're mad."

"You haven't been around my family." I liked that I'd made her laugh. It was a good sound.

"You're obviously close." She tossed the washcloth in the sink. "Um…Gwen did say that you'd only known Zach for a few months. She said that was her fault."

"It was my fault as much as hers." I didn't like talking about it…but I didn't like her thinking I was the kind of bastard who'd ignore his son, either. "I didn't know about Zach's existence until last March. Gwen and I met when I was on vacation a few years ago. It didn't work out—at least, I decided it wouldn't work out. She has money, you see. Family money. A lot of it. I didn't deal with that well when I found out. She, uh, threw away my address when I left, so by the time she realized she was pregnant, she didn't know how to find me."

"How did you learn about Zach, then?"

"She hired a detective. That was after she'd been diagnosed with breast cancer." I added firmly, so she'd know the subject was closed, "She's okay now. Anyway, she brought Zach here for a visit, and while Zach and I were getting acquainted, she and Duncan fell for each other."

They'd fought it. In hindsight I could see that it must have been hell for both of them. They'd known I'd wanted to marry Gwen, and Duncan at least had accepted that I had a prior claim. But at the time I hadn't been able to see anything except how betrayed I'd felt when I found out, how thoroughly my dreams had been destroyed.

Seely rested her hand on my knee. "I'm glad you told me. If Zach is going to be here often, I wouldn't want to say or do the wrong thing."

That was a good reason for having shot off my mouth. Not the real reason, maybe, but while we were on the subject…. "You should probably know something else. If Zach starts talking about the bad man and the policeman who shot him—well, that really happened. Maybe someone filled you in on that?"

They hadn't. Useless bunch of busybodies. Why hadn't they told her the stuff that mattered, so I wouldn't have to? I didn't like thinking about that night. The strobing red of the cop car lights, the hard white light inside the store, where a crazy bastard had held Gwen and my son at gunpoint…the fear, raw and jagged like a gutful of broken glass.

I'd failed them. No matter how often I told myself there was nothing I could have done to protect them, the bitterness of my failure didn't go away.

But Seely would need to know the basics, so I told her about the holdup of a convenience store last April, and how Gwen and Zach had been among the hostages taken by a not-too-bright gunman. And how Duncan had saved them.

"My God, Ben. You said something about Zach having had a lot of uncertainty in his life, but I never imagined anything like this."

"He seems to be doing okay. Gwen took him to this guy who does play therapy. That's where kids tell their stories with toys," I explained, "and the therapist sort of plays with them, only in a way that helps them work through things."

"What about you?"

"I wasn't part of it."

"That's what I mean. There's nothing worse than being helpless when someone you love is hurting or in danger."

Uncomfortable, I said, "I don't usually blather on so much. I just thought you ought to know."

She chuckled. "You call that blathering? I don't think anything you said even qualifies as a secret. And I do know a few. It's amazing what people will say to a paramedic. I suppose doctors and nurses experience that, too."

Was that why I felt like there was something between us—because she'd saved my life? Turning the idea over in my mind, I decided it made sense.

She stood. "Seems to me you could use some play therapy yourself, but for now we'll settle for getting you dressed. C'mon, up with you. I'll take that sling off."

The moment I stood, the room shrank. Seely was standing very close, and the soft herbal scent of her hair seemed stronger. I pretended I didn't notice. "I can get this strap in front."

"Okay. Turn a bit…there." The sling came loose, and she slipped it off. "Of course, I don't know half the secrets Daisy does. If you ever met her, you'd find yourself telling her your life story in no time. People do."

My shoulder ached more without the sling's support, so I supported that arm with my other hand. "Who's Daisy? A friend?"

"That, yes. Also my mother."

"You call your mother by her first name?"

"Sure. Can you get those buttons, or do you need some help?"

I thought about letting her unbutton my pajama shirt. Her knuckles would brush against my skin…better to let my right arm dangle and fumble the buttons out left-handed. "I can do it. You did say your mother was unusual."

She chuckled again. A man could get hooked on that sound. "Unusual, yes. She used to be a flower child. The real thing, Haight-Ashbury and all that. In some ways she still is, though she's doing pretty well as an artist these days. I tease her that she's lost in the sixties. Here, we'll do the difficult arm first."

She eased the pajama shirt off my shoulder. It fit snugly over the bandages, so she had to take her time. It was ridiculous to get turned on by that, under the circumstances. But it was a good thing the sweatpants were baggy. "An artist, huh? What kind?"

"Sculpture. She's into what she calls found art these days. Some people call it junk—" her grin flashed "—but she's had two showings at a prestigious gallery in Taos. She scavenges for things people throw away, then paints this or that, puts the objects together and ends up with some pretty interesting pieces."

"Real modern stuff, I take it."

"Well, one critic called it 'an entrancing collision between the primitive and the twenty-first century,' but yes. I have a sneaking suspicion it wouldn't be your type of art." She tossed the pajama shirt on the back of the toilet, then picked up the flannel shirt she'd brought down earlier.

"What about your father? What does he do?"

"Who knows? He came down with a bad case of respectability a few years after I was born. Poor man. I don't think he ever recovered. Here, hold out your arm."

She didn't say anything else while I eased my right arm slowly into a sleeve, then my left. This gave me plenty of time to kick myself. She'd mentioned her mother several times, her father not at all. That should have clued me in.

"I know your shoulder is hurting," she said cheerily. "Turn around and let me do up the buttons. That way you can support that arm until we get the sling back on."

I did turn, but ignored the rest of her instructions. "Sometimes I don't watch where I'm putting my big feet. I stepped in the wrong place. I'm sorry."

Her eyes flicked to mine, surprised. Then a wry smile tipped her lips. "Ben, you're supposed to pretend there's nothing beneath my flip attitude but more flip."

"I'm not much good at pretending."

"No, you aren't," she said so gently she seemed to be touching on some great secret. "I think I like that about you."

She liked my voice, too. And I liked all sorts of things about her. My gaze drifted to her mouth. "I can't imagine what it would be like to grow up with so little family. I'm used to a crowd."

"But you were a lot older than the others, weren't you? You said Duncan is the closest to you in age, and he's five years younger. That's not a big difference now, but it would have been when you were growing up. You wouldn't have played together, or gone on double dates when you were teens, or—oh, all the things an only child thinks siblings are for."

"No, but that's not…they mattered. I mean, it mattered that they were around, that…hell. I don't know how to say it."

"Maybe that they were a huge part of your life? And you love them."

I nodded, relieved that she understood. "I'm not great with words."

"I think you do pretty well." She paused, then went on quietly, "I haven't seen or spoken to my father since I was eight. Um…he and Daisy weren't married."

I felt privileged, as if she'd handed me a private little piece of herself that she didn't leave lying around where just anyone might see it. "He missed a lot, then. Practically everything that matters."

"He did, didn't he?" Her smile slid back in place. "More than me, because I had Daisy."

"The two of you are close?"

She nodded, then just stood there looking up at me, curiosity and something else in those incredible eyes.

It occurred to me that I wouldn't have to bend far to taste her smile.

My heartbeat picked up. I could see the pulse beating in the hollow of her throat, too. Maybe she was having the same thoughts I was. Maybe she wanted me to kiss her. That sweet notion had my head dipping toward hers.

Had I lost my ever-loving *mind?*

Reality snapped back in place. So did my head. Panicked, trying to cover up the moment, I fumbled for the buttons of my shirt.

I forgot that I couldn't use my right arm.

"Oh, damn—*sit!*" She enforced the order with a shove.

I sat. I didn't have enough breath to curse, much less protest.

"You are *not* going to pass out on me," she informed me.

"Of course not." The first hard smack of pain had passed, but my forehead felt clammy. I cleared my throat. "I should probably get the sling back on so I don't forget and try to use that arm again."

"Probably," she said dryly, and retrieved the sling. Our conversation after that consisted of her instructions to me— turn, hold your arm out, that sort of thing. Did she know I'd been about to kiss her? I couldn't tell.

I fastened the straps myself. "I need to call Manny. He's good, but he's not used to overseeing everything."

She studied my face a moment. "Sure. As long as you call him from bed."

I scowled. "The couch in the living room—"

The doorbell rang. It must have woken Doofus; I heard his excited yips and the scrabble of his claws on the floor outside the bathroom as he skidded around the corner, heading for the entry hall.

Seely glanced over her shoulder, then back at me. "Stay put. I'll be back to help you in a minute." She left the bathroom.

I considered the ethics of my situation. I was supposed to

do what she said, but there was that "within reason" clause I'd stuck on. She hadn't stayed around to hear my reasons for not staying put.

One, I wasn't dizzy anymore. Two, the foyer was just the other side of the bathroom. Three, I wanted to see who was here.

I reached for the walking stick.

It was slow and awkward, but the cane did help. Seely was just shutting the front door when I got there, holding Doofus back with her foot so the little idiot didn't scamper out and get into the street. She turned around, tossing a set of keys up and catching them one-handed. Temper sparked in her eyes.

I had a good guess who'd been at the door.

All of a sudden she said, "Here!" And tossed the keys at me.

To catch them, I'd have to drop the walking stick. I let them sail on past. They landed with a rattle on the hardwood floor. Doofus trotted over to investigate them. "Did you miss me on purpose, or was that a happy accident?"

She looked at me like I was something the cat had hacked up on the rug. "The mechanic I took my car to just left."

I nodded, having figured out that much. "All fixed, I take it."

"Against my explicit instructions—yes!" Those sparks turned into big, blazing fires. "That man—that weaselly, low-life scum I'd *thought* was an honest mechanic—he wouldn't even tell me what the repairs had cost. Just winked at me, handed me the keys and said it was all taken care of. He practically patted my hand and told me not to worry my pretty little head!"

"Well, then. Looks like you can stop worrying."

She growled. Honest to God, that's what it sounded like. "This is not worry. This is *fury*." She stalked closer, tilting her face to snarl up at me, "You paid for it. You went behind my back and paid for the whole thing."

"I wasn't going to let you lose your car. You saved my life."

"You had no right! No right at all! You didn't even ask me!"

"If I'd asked," I pointed out, "you probably would have argued. I'm sure that wouldn't be good for me, weak as I am right now."

"It wouldn't be good for you if I were to trip you, either. Or poison your coffee. Or—or—dammit, if you don't stop grinning at me in that obnoxious way, I'm going to do something we'll both regret!"

I was grinning, wasn't I? Once she'd called attention to that, my grin widened. I was enjoying myself. A lot. Seely in a temper was something to see—eyes hot, cheeks flushed, those volatile eyebrows drawn down in a scowl. So, like the daredevil I'd never been, I plunged off the next cliff. "You are cute as hell when you're mad, you know that?"

Her mouth dropped open. It closed and opened a couple more times before she got some words out. "That knock on the head did more damage than the doctor realized."

"A lot like a kitten—hissing, scratching, growling. Cute."

"I am five feet, ten and a half inches tall in my stocking feet. I am not *cute*. And you are obviously mentally as well as physically handicapped, so I suppose I shouldn't hit you too hard."

"Well, if you're already planning on hitting me…" I said that, so on some level I must have known what I was about to do. But the thought never got up to the top of my brain where I could squash it. Something else was pulling my strings, as if some part of me I'd never known existed was suddenly in charge.

I let the walking stick clatter to the floor, cupped the back of her head and kissed her.

Her lips were soft. That wasn't a surprise. She went rigid the second my mouth touched hers. No surprise there, either. But the kick of pleasure went deeper than I'd expected. The taste of her shot straight to the primitive part of my brain the way smells do, bypassing reason. I couldn't have known that would happen. And there's no way I could have predicted the funny little sound she made just before she melted up against me.

One of us was still thinking, I guess, because she was careful of my shoulder, sliding one arm around me and letting her other hand rest on my waist. I hummed my approval against those soft lips, threaded my fingers through her hair and tilted her head so I could deepen the kiss. And she opened for me.

Automatically I widened my stance so I could snug her up closer. The stupid sling was in the way and my knee protested, but the way her fingers kneaded my waist mattered a lot more.

So did the warm, living feel of her beneath my hand. I loved the fact that I didn't have to bend over much to explore the flavors inside her mouth, and the way she stroked her tongue along mine. The long muscles of her back invited me to sample the dip at her waist, the smooth curve of her bottom.

She liked my body, too. Her hand left my waist to range up beneath my shirt and over my chest. Delight slid into need without a bump to mark the change.

I slid my right leg between hers and pressed up. She shivered. I needed more, needed her skin, her sighs, the little bud of her nipple in my mouth…where? Where could I take her? The living room was close, and the couch there was long and roomy. I started easing us both that way without taking my mouth from hers.

My foot slid out from under me.

I yelled. Doofus yipped. Seely's arm tightened around me, and somehow I managed not to fall on my stupid ass.

Not literally, anyway. Appalled by my behavior, I yanked

my hand away and stepped back. My heartbeat was doing the hundred-yard dash, my knee hurt, my shoulder hurt, and my foot was…wet. I glanced down.

"Oh," Seely said, one hand rising to her mouth to smother a giggle. She crouched to pet the droopy-eared puppy. "Oh, Doofus. You did *try* to go out, didn't you, boy?"

Saved from my own worst self by a puppy's bladder. Mortified, I said stiffly, "I apologize. I said you wouldn't have to deal with, uh, grabby hands, and then…all I can do is apologize, and promise it won't happen again."

Her gaze took a lazy trip up me while she fondled the puppy's ears. She made a tch-ing sound, shook her head and stood. "Didn't your sister ever tell you? Never apologize to a woman for kissing her—not if she kissed you back."

My ears felt hot. The rest of me was sore, aroused, exhausted and bewildered. "The last employer who made a pass at you ended up wearing someone else's dinner."

"Ben." Her smile started in her eyes and glowed its way down to her mouth. She patted my cheek. "You're not Vic, are you?"

She turned away, picked up my walking stick and handed it to me. "What you should be apologizing for is interfering in my arrangements with the mechanic. I suppose your intentions were good, but it was intolerably high-handed. How much did the repairs cost?"

"I don't know yet, and it doesn't matter."

"Probably not," she agreed easily, turning away. "Since I doubt I'd be able to repay you. I'd better get something to clean up that puddle."

"You don't have to repay me. I don't want you to."

She headed for the kitchen. "As far as I'm concerned, the car is yours now. I'll get the title switched over as soon as possible."

I frowned. Her threat about the car was annoying, but not

a real problem. If she put it in my name, I'd just put it back in hers. A much bigger worry was my own behavior.

My sister, Annie, has accused me of seeing everything in black-and-white. Maybe I do. But right and wrong have never seemed all that complicated, and if a man knows what's right, that's what he should do. Even when it's hard. Maybe especially then.

Kissing Seely was wrong. I knew that, even if she didn't. She was an employee. She was also a warm, giving sort of woman who deserved better than hand-me-downs from a man in love with another woman.

I knew that. So why had I kissed her?

No answers floated up. I stood there, aware of a number of places that hurt, and the lingering hum of arousal that defied the pain. After a moment I sighed and limped for the bathroom.

There was one bright spot. I'd stepped in the blasted puddle with my right foot, not my left. At least I could wash it myself.

Five

"**D**oes it hurt a lot?" Zach asked.

"Not anymore."

"How much does it hurt? This much?" He used his thumb and forefinger to take a tiny pinch of air. "Or this much?" He held out both hands broadly.

"About like this." I measured a couple of inches between my finger and thumb. "More at bedtime, because I'm tired."

He nodded seriously. "When I'm sick I hurt more at bedtime. How does this thing go on?" He pointed at my sling.

We were sitting on the rear deck, enjoying what was probably one of the last warm afternoons of the year. Zach was perched on my right thigh. My left foot was propped up on a little table to keep the knee elevated. That had been Seely's idea, keeping the knee elevated, and I guess it did help. The swelling had gone down some. Doofus lay nearby, panting hopefully.

I showed Zach how my sling fastened, undoing one of the Velcro tapes and letting him restick it a few times. Velcro was one of Zach's favorite things. He wanted to know if he could have the sling to play with after I was all better.

I smiled. "Sure." God only knew what he planned to do with it. That didn't matter. The important thing was that he'd accepted I would be "all better" eventually.

He told me Doofus was lonely and clambered down to play with his pup. I handed him his magnifying glass—another of his favorite things—and pup and boy ran off to look for bugs. My throat closed up as I watched them. I'd come so close to never having an afternoon like this again.

On the other side of the sliding glass doors behind me, Seely was chopping things in the kitchen and talking to Gwen. The two of them seemed to have really hit it off. That was undoubtedly a good thing, but it made me uncomfortable. Women tell each other the damnedest things sometimes.

I couldn't stop thinking about that kiss.

Not that I thought about it every second. I had plenty of other things on my mind, like reassuring Zach, trying to set up the remodel job at the resort without leaving the house, and problems on the Pearson site.

But the memory of that kiss kept ambushing me.

I'd been eating lunch—Seely had made cheeseburgers—and all of a sudden I'd noticed her hands, the long fingers and short nails, and I'd remembered how she'd dug those fingers into my back. When Doofus tried to trip me on the way to the bathroom, I thought about how he'd nearly caused another accident.

Shoot, in the middle of a crossword puzzle the word *erupt* made me think of volcanoes, lava and heat, and I was right back with that kiss. All day long, it kept popping out at me like a jack-in-the-box with a broken lid.

I didn't like it. It's not that I expect to control my thoughts a hundred percent of the time, but I don't like being pushed around by them, either.

Maybe hiring Seely hadn't been such a great idea. I was stuck with the decision, though. It wouldn't be fair to change my mind now. I'd just have to get myself up to par as quickly as possible so I could let her go.

And then she wouldn't be off-limits anymore.

That sneaky thought annoyed me. I drummed my fingers on the arm of the chair. Once Seely's employment with me was over, she probably wouldn't be in Highpoint anymore, either. Duncan had found her at the bus station, for God's sake. And I wasn't interested in trying to persuade a reluctant woman to stay. I'd failed miserably the last time.

My chest tightened. That twitchy, brittle feeling climbed over me, the one that had ridden me too often lately, as if I were wearing my skin backward. One wrong move could split it, spilling all sorts of messy, inner bits out on the dirty ground. Yet I craved motion, action.

I was scared.

I'd wanted Gwen, wanted her for keeps. I'd gone at getting her to marry me the way I go after any important goal, giving it everything I had. And I'd flopped, big-time. She'd fallen for my brother.

Plenty of times in the last few months I'd told myself I needed to start looking for a woman to share my life. And hadn't done it. I'd begun to wonder what was wrong with me, if maybe I was too old to marry for the first time. Maybe my standards were too high, or there was something missing in me. Maybe I'd missed my chance for a family of my own.

For a long, still moment, I sat there in my wicker chair on

the deck I'd built and faced a truth I'd been dodging. Deep down, I wasn't sure I could handle failing again.

The late-afternoon sunshine hit the yard at a strong slant, dragging long shadows from the poplars along the back fence that striped the yard in plump diagonals. I hadn't mowed the grass in three weeks. It was still green but had stopped growing. The leaves on the oak showed more gold than green in the autumn sun.

By the back gate, Zach and Doofus were digging industriously. I smiled, wondering what he was digging for. Gold? Diamonds? Or the sheer joy of making a nice, big hole in the ground?

Maybe it wouldn't be so bad if I never managed to pull off the wife-and-family bit. I had Zach. I didn't have him every day, but lots of fathers were in that position these days. Didn't they say that happiness lay in being content with what you have, instead of yearning for more?

My fingers started drumming again. To hell with that. Sounded like giving up to me.

The doors behind me slid open, and a wonderful aroma drifted out.

"Thought you might like some sweet tea," Seely said. "It's a Southern tradition."

"Sure. Thanks." I accepted the glass she held out, willing to try one of her traditions. "I don't need that jacket, Gwen."

Seely took the old rocker. Gwen sat in the wicker chair that matched mine, laying my jacket across her knees. "If you say so. You know me—I'm always cold." She studied my face a moment. "You're right, Seely. He does look better. Hard to believe he's actually been behaving."

"I don't know why everyone thinks I'm incapable of taking care of myself. I've been doing it for a few years now." I took a sip of tea. "This is good. So, I guess the two of you have been, uh, getting acquainted?"

Gwen shook her head, grinning. "The look on your face, Ben! It's easy to see you think the two of us had nothing better to talk about than you. Shame on you."

"You've been talking for over an hour. In my experience, that's enough time for two women to exchange their life histories and get started on everyone else's."

Seely laughed. The rocker creaked as she leaned forward to pat my knee. "Don't worry. She didn't spill the beans about your misspent youth."

Gwen frowned. "I don't think Ben *had* a misspent youth. Or much of a youth at all, with the way he had to give up everything when…" Her voice trailed off. Maybe because of the look on my face.

The rocking chair creaked again as Seely leaned back. "Actually, we talked about your house more than you. I love old houses."

"Yeah?" I relaxed, pleased. "This one isn't all that old compared to some back east. But around here, homes over fifty years old aren't common."

"When was it built?"

"In 1935, but my grandfather used salvaged pieces from older houses where he could. That's fashionable now, but not too many people were doing it back then. The wainscoting in the entry and the mantel in the living room are about 120 years old. Came from an old bawdy house."

She laughed. "Oh, that's wonderful! And the staircase? That looks old."

"The newel post is over a hundred years old."

"It's a grand old house." She rocked gently a moment. "A pity it's neglected, but I suppose that's like the cobbler's children going barefoot. You're probably too busy building other people's homes to have time for your own."

I sat up straight. "What the hell are you talking about? Everything's in great shape!"

"I'm sure it is. Maybe *neglected* was the wrong word. It just doesn't look like anything has changed much in twenty years."

I had my mouth open, ready to blast her, when Zach came running up, chanting his mom-mom-mom mantra.

"Good grief, you're dirty," Gwen said.

"Yeah. Come see the bug me an' Doofus found. You, too, Seely," he said, politely including her in the treat. He and she had settled it earlier that he was to use her first name. "It's tre-*men*-duz."

Lots of things were tre-*men*-duz lately. I reached for my stick.

Seely stood, put her hand on my good shoulder and asked, with one lifted eyebrow, if I was sure I ought to get up. I scowled at her, but stayed put. "The steps from the deck are tricky for me," I told Zach. "I'll sit this bug out."

Everyone else headed across the yard. Over by the rear gate, Doofus was barking at the pile of dirt he and Zach had created. I assume the bug was there. Seely grinned at Zach and said something I couldn't make out. Zach giggled. Gwen smiled at him, then tilted her head to speak to Seely.

Seen side by side, the two women couldn't have looked more different. Gwen was a tidy little thing, her short hair pale and shiny in the sunlight. Seely was at least a head taller. More robust. Brighter, somehow.

I frowned. More irritating, too. What was so great about changing stuff around, anyway? Everything worked. And it wasn't as if I hadn't done anything to the place for twenty years. The couch and area rug in the living room were only five years old. Of course, it was Annie who'd nagged me into replacing them, but so what? And maybe they sat in exactly the same spot as the old ones had, but they looked good there.

The deck I was sitting on—I'd added that myself.

Fifteen years ago.

Doofus suddenly tried to catch his tail, and Seely laughed. She had a husky laugh. It made me think of a messy bed, with the sheets dripping to the floor and Seely rising above me, throwing her hair back and laughing just like that…

Whoa. That was weird, fantasizing about Seely with Gwen right next to her. But guilt was stupid. I owed Gwen family loyalty, and that was all. I was allowed to look at other women. In fact, I'd damned well better start looking.

First, though, I had to finish healing. Right now I couldn't even pick a woman up to take her to dinner. I sighed, thinking of my truck. I needed to find out what kind of hoops the insurance company wanted me to jump through before they'd issue a check.

The phone was sitting on the table beside me. I'd brought it out because I'd been talking to Manny earlier. I'd input dozens of numbers into the directory when I bought the phone a few months ago.

Not everything around here was old, dammit.

Bah. I punched up the directory. Time to put my brain to some kind of *productive* use.

Gwen slid Zach's arm into a jacket he didn't really need. "Seely, it was a pleasure meeting you. No, Ben, sit down. Don't walk to the car with us."

I shook my head sadly as I used the walking stick to lever myself upright. "What is it about me being injured that turns everyone into tyrant wannabes?"

Seely chuckled, Gwen grimaced, and Zach wanted to know why he couldn't take his bug home. To prove I could compromise, I limped to the door with them instead of going all the way to the car. "I guess I'll see you Saturday, kid." I ruffled the top of Zach's head.

He looked puzzled. "Are you goin', too?"

"Oh, Lord." Gwen rolled her eyes. "I can't believe I forgot to tell you. Duncan was going to when he stopped by yesterday, but you were sleeping."

"Tell me what?"

"Zach was terribly disappointed about missing out on his camping trip with you. Duncan managed to get some time off so he could take him."

The knife slid in so fast I couldn't guard against it. *I* was supposed to be the one who took Zach camping and hiking. I was the one who'd taught Duncan, dammit. Not to mention Charlie and Annie. Our parents hadn't much cared about that sort of thing, but I did. I always had.

My brother had everything else—why did he have to grab this, too?

"Dad?" Zach sounded uncertain.

So I smiled. "Just feeling sorry for myself because I have to miss this one. But you can tell me all about it when you get back, right?"

"Right!"

I didn't watch them drive away. I never do. That's a rule. Every time Zach leaves—especially when Gwen picks him up—I get hit with a load of might-have-beens. No point in taking a chance on Zach guessing how I felt. Kids often blame themselves when the adults in their lives are screwing up.

But I did wait to shut the door until they were both in Gwen's car.

Seely was standing behind me. "That was hard," she said. "You handled it well."

I grunted, annoyed with her for seeing too much, and hobbled toward the living room. "Not that hard. My knee's doing better."

"I wasn't talking about your knee. But I think you know that and are trying delicately to hint me away from the subject. Unfortunately," she said sadly, "I am almost immune to hints."

A quick snort of laughter snuck out before I could stop it. "That's the first time anyone's ever called me delicate. I hear blunt, rude, pigheaded and tactless from time to time, but not delicate."

"There you go. We have a lot in common. I figure you'll understand how hard it is for a basically direct person to tiptoe around a subject. Much easier to just say what you're thinking, isn't it?"

"Gets you in trouble sometimes," I said. I'd reached the couch and sat down, suppressing a sigh of relief. Stupid knee. My shoulder wasn't feeling too great, either.

"Trouble can be interesting. Here, let me help you get that leg up."

"I can do it."

"Now how did I know you were going to say that?" She ignored my scowl, putting her hands under my calf and helping me lift the leg onto the couch. "I must be psychic."

"That makes sense. It's not like I'm predictable."

She laughed and settled on the other end, curling one leg up beneath her. That surprised me. She'd mostly stayed away this afternoon unless I needed something…which I figured was my fault. Because of that kiss. With my leg stretched out between us, I couldn't jump her. That's probably what she was thinking.

And I was not thinking about that kiss again. I was just wondering if she was.

"I liked watching you and Zach together," she said. "Gave me the idea that you're crazy about him."

"Well, yeah. Of course I am. Any man… " My voice trailed off as I remembered that her father hadn't acted like he was crazy about her. I cleared my throat. "Of course, some men are jerks."

"I can agree with that."

The bitter note in her voice surprised me, though it shouldn't have. She had a right to be bitter. "Do you hate him?" I asked abruptly. "Your father, I mean."

She blinked. "I…oh, damn, I wanted to say no, that he doesn't matter enough to hate. And that's almost true. But sometimes…"

She shrugged and looked away, but not before I'd seen the unhappiness in her eyes. "It's like having a trick knee. You go along fine for days, weeks, even months. Then all of a sudden you put your weight on it, and it doesn't hold. Every now and then I still get angry. Dumb, isn't it?" Her mouth twisted. "I'm thirty-two years old. I should be over it by now."

"I don't see what 'should' has to do with it. Seems to me we can control our actions, but thoughts and feelings don't pay much attention to rules." Or I wouldn't be thinking about that blasted kiss again.

She looked startled, then smiled. "I suspect a lot of people underestimate you."

That was probably a compliment. I studied her a moment. Though her body was easy, relaxed, I thought shadows lingered in her eyes. I decided to steer us into less painful territory. "So, what would you change in here?"

"Me?"

"You said things hadn't been changed in a long time. You must have had something in mind."

"I'd paint the walls," she said promptly.

I looked around critically. "Nothing wrong with the paint."

"It's white, Ben."

"So?"

"So the room could use some color. Red would be great."

"You're kidding."

"Green would be good, too—a rich green, nothing wimpy. But this couch is a lovely, warm brown. I think red would be great with it. And maybe some molding over the fireplace to match the crown moldings. That would make the mantel really pop."

I eyed her dubiously. "You sound like an upscale decorator."

She laughed. "I'll admit to being hooked on those shows on cable."

"They have decorating shows?"

"Don't watch much TV, do you?"

"Not if I can help it."

"Well, there's a whole network devoted to it. Shows about gardening and all kinds of decorating—window treatments, kitchen remodels, painting techniques, all that sort of thing." She grinned. "A friend of mine calls it female porn. We can look and drool, but we can't touch."

"Sounds about right." I gave a thoughtful nod. "Green, maybe. I could see a pale green in here. Or purple."

"Uh…purple?"

"Sure. Put a little gilding on the crown moldings, too. It would really dress the place up."

She caught on. "Gilding the moldings! I never would have thought of that. But then, you really must use red for the walls. Chinese red. And maybe a little pagoda in the corner?"

We spent the next few minutes turning my living room into a Chinese emperor's nightmare, complete with bamboo, lacquered screens and dragons, all in the most garish cast of colors possible. Somehow that evolved into a discussion of building styles, remodeling and how to honor the architectural integrity of a building when creating an addition.

Now, all this was right up my alley. I don't often swing a hammer or hang drywall myself these days, but I've done it enough in the past. A good builder has to know a little about everything, from the right temperature to pour concrete to the current craze for paint glazes to how to shore up a damaged load-bearing wall. So it might seem like I was enjoying some shop talk and Seely was humoring me, but it wasn't like that. It wasn't about me at all. I would have talked about blueberry muffin recipes if that's what got her this excited, just so I could watch her glow.

This slow-moving woman came alive when she talked houses. Which was downright peculiar for a woman with no nesting urges.

"Your den is an addition, isn't it?" she said. She was snuggled into the corner of the couch, her shoes off and her feet tucked up. A strand of hair had worked loose to wiggle along her temple and cheekbone like a hyperactive question mark.

I grimaced. "Sticks out like a sore thumb, doesn't it? I've always meant to redo it. The roofline messes up the rear and side elevations. My father had it done, and I don't think he gave a thought to how it fit with the rest of the house's style."

"He wasn't interested in construction and architecture himself, then?"

"Sure, if it took place two or three thousand years ago."

"I've wondered about that," she said slowly. "I would have thought there would be exotic mementos scattered around from all the time he spent abroad. Pot shards, maybe, or a scarab or two."

"I've got a pretty little Egyptian lady in my bedroom, on the dresser. Most of that stuff is boxed up, though. Never really knew what to do with it. Now what," I demanded, "did I say to put that polite look on your face?"

"Who, me? Polite?"

"Like you're thinking something you're too nice to say."

"Oh." She flushed. "And here I'm trying to be tactful…it just seems like you have some issues with your parents. Maybe with the way they died and left you to raise the family they'd started."

My good mood evaporated. "I did what had to be done. That's all."

"And that was a less-than-delicate hint to close the subject. Good enough." She said that with perfect good humor, but rose to her feet. "I'd better go check on the roast."

"Don't rush off. I didn't mean to…dammit, you can't get offended every time I'm an ass, or we won't be able to talk at all."

She patted my shoulder. "No offense taken. I don't blame you for getting testy when people make a fuss about the way you took on the responsibility for your brothers and sisters. It must seem sometimes as if you're defined by what happened twenty years ago. As if nothing you've done since then matters, compared to that."

Having leveled me with a few words, she swayed gently toward the door. "Supper should be ready soon. You want to eat on a tray in here?"

I must have answered, because she left the room. God only knows what I said. I don't know how long I sat staring at the wall and seeing nothing, either.

Eventually sheer physical discomfort roused me. My shoulder this time. I mushed some pillows around to create more support for it, leaned back and waited for the fire to die down.

The blasted woman had a bad habit of saying outrageous things, then wandering off, leaving me no one to argue with but myself. That would stop, I promised myself. If she was going to drop bombshells, she could damned well hang around and deal with the debris.

But Seely wasn't in the habit of hanging around.

Never mind. People could change, right? She was big on changing walls and furniture. She could just get used to the idea of changing a couple of habits, too.

It was a helluva thing, but somewhere between Chinese-red walls and that irritating pat on my shoulder, my gut had made a decision without consulting the rest of me. For the next few days, I'd be such a good patient my family would worry about me.

Because I had to get well and fire Seely. Soon. I was going to have that woman out of my employ—and in my bed.

Six

The next day, Manny came over for lunch. He dropped off the paint we'd chosen and some painting equipment, then helped Seely move the furniture out of the living room.

I can't explain how I came to agree to this. Slippery, that's what she is. She started out by acting as if I'd already agreed. I recognized this trick, since Annie used to pull it. She'd get me to agree that music is important, mention that she wanted to spend the night with a friend, then pretend that meant I'd agreed to let her go to a concert in Denver with that friend.

When I explained Annie's teenage tricks to Seely, she looked thoughtful and said she really needed to meet my sister. The next thing I knew we were discussing paint colors.

I did protest. She wasn't being paid to paint my house, for God's sake. And I couldn't help her. She wouldn't have let me, for one thing. I couldn't pretend it would be unreasonable to forbid me to paint the living room, so I was bound by our agreement.

But that did not make it reasonable for her to do it, either. I asked if she'd ever done any painting.

"Not a lick," she'd said cheerfully. "We'll pull the couch into the middle of the room. You can lie there and supervise."

Sage green. That's the color we ended up with.

I sat on the couch with my bad leg stretched out, and scowled as Manny and Seely carried the last of the chairs into the dining room. Supervising didn't suit me nearly as well as everyone seemed to think.

"You sure you don't want me to help with the prep?" Manny was asking her as they rejoined me. "Or move the rest of the junk out?" He jerked a thumb over his shoulder in my direction.

"I'm sure I can work around the couch."

"Wasn't talking about the couch."

Seely's lips twitched.

"Manny thinks he's a wit," I mentioned. "You might not be able to tell, since his face muscles atrophied years ago. That's the only expression he's got."

Manny has an evil chuckle, like a machine gun misfiring. He employed it as he headed for the front door, advising Seely in between bursts not to let me give her a hard time. He paused in the arched entry. "Meant to tell you—that doctor called this morning."

"What doctor?"

"The one that put you back together in the E.R."

"Oh," Gwen said. "The idiot."

Manny fired another couple of bursts. "That's the one. He seemed to think you'd hurt your shoulder a few days ago instead of when you drove off a mountain. Wanted me to confirm that." He shook his head. "Weird guy."

"Yeah." I frowned as Seely walked Manny to the door. Harry Meckle was weird, but he wasn't really an idiot. Just the opposite.

The doorbell rang. I heard them talking to someone else at the door and reached for my walking stick.

"Stay put," Seely called. "It's just a delivery."

I sighed and put the stick down. A moment later I heard the door shut, then she came back into the room carrying a box. "I like Manny. I wish you'd told me, though. I'm afraid I stared at first."

"What? Oh. That's right—you hadn't met him in person." In addition to being a pain in the butt, a master electrician and the best foreman I've ever had, Manny is a dwarf. "I didn't think about it. To me he's just Manny."

She handed me the box, treating me to that slow smile. "Not 'Manny the dwarf.' Just Manny."

"Well, yeah." The logo was printed in the corner, so I knew what it held. I didn't want to open it now. "You know how it is. Once you know someone, you don't see them the same way." I decided to give her a hint. "There should be a screw-driver in the toolbox. You'll want to remove the switch plates first."

"I was hoping for a tool belt." She bent and rummaged through the toolbox. "I'm sure I'd feel more competent with a tool belt."

My lips twitched. Picturing a tool belt slung around those thoroughly female hips didn't make me think of competence.

Seely ambled over to the entry and began unfastening the switch plate there. "You like to read, don't you? I noticed that your bookshelves are heavy on history."

It turned out that Seely enjoyed history, too, though she was a slow reader. A mild case of dyslexia, she said, made a book a major investment of time for her. She considered herself lucky, since she'd been diagnosed early, and talked about a teacher who'd helped her. When I asked, she claimed paramedic training hadn't been too hard. It might take her a while to read something, but, as with many dyslexics, she had an excellent memory.

Though she usually leaned more toward historical fiction than the straight stuff, she asked if I could recommend something on American history "without too many battles," since she was more interested in people than military action.

I did, of course, and invited her to borrow my copy. By then she'd finished taping off the woodwork and was prying open the paint. She poured it into the pan. "Oh, look! Isn't that luscious?"

I looked. She'd taken the drapes down already, so light from the two tall windows flooded the room. The old pair of painter's coveralls I'd found for her completely obscured that glorious figure; her exuberant hair was braided tightly away from her face.

Which glowed. Not in an unearthly way, though. With pure delight. "Luscious," I agreed.

Maybe I did know how I'd ended up agreeing to let her paint the room, after all.

As she spread great, sweeping strokes of sage green across my walls, I found myself telling her how I'd come to enjoy reading so much. I didn't miss the architectural career I might have had; the hands-on business of construction suited me. But abandoning college before I could get my degree had nagged at me, as if I'd drawn most of a circle and never finished that last arc. So I'd started reading the kinds of things I thought would complete my education. In the process, I discovered a taste for history.

"It's full of great stories," she agreed, stepping back to survey her work. The roller work was almost done; next came the nit-picky brush work. "Daisy says we have to know where we come from to understand where we are."

"Your mother sounds like a bright woman. You missed a spot up by the ceiling in the west corner," I pointed out politely.

She glanced at me over her shoulder. "You're enjoying this."

"Who'd have thought it?" I shook my head in amazement. "I never tried sitting around watching someone else work. I like it." Especially when she bent over and the coveralls stretched tight across her round, lovely bottom.

She'd ordered me to stay on the couch. I doubt she was thinking about me making a quick tackle, then rolling her onto her back on the drop cloth. I was, though. Never mind that I'd probably have passed out if I'd tried. It was just as well that our agreement kept me from pitting common sense against the irrational optimism of lust.

Seely got the spot I'd pointed out, then stretched...an inspiring sight. "So what do you think? Will it need a second coat?"

I made myself take a good look at the walls. "Hey," I said slowly. "This looks good. Really good."

"It does, doesn't it?" She put her hands on her hips, surveying her work. The streak of green paint along her jaw curled up at one end, as smug as her smile. "Though I still say red would have worked, the green looks great. Refreshing."

She'd brought me some paint chips to choose from that morning. I'd held out for a lighter, warmer shade than she wanted, being more familiar with translating the way a color looked on a tiny chip to an entire room. "You were right about the room needing color."

"Well!" Her eyebrows rose. "A man who can admit he was wrong. Color me amazed."

"You have brothers," I muttered. "Or used to. You probably murdered them and buried the bodies."

She let out a peal of laughter. "Watch it, or you'll end up with a green nose."

"To match yours?"

She lifted a hand to her nose. The bracelet she never removed slid down her arm. "It isn't…"

"It is now."

"I must look like a little girl who's been finger painting."

"No," I said slowly. "You look like an uncommonly beautiful woman. Only *slightly* green."

The smile she turned on me was different. Hesitant.

"Why have you never married, Seely?"

Her smile faded, as if it were on a dimmer switch and I'd just turned it down. "You're changing the rules on me. Feeling safe, are you, over there on the couch?"

My heart began to pound. I didn't have to figure out what she meant. "Not safe at all. You?"

She shook her head and bent to get the narrow brush I'd told her to use around the baseboards. She took the brush and the paint tray over to the window and settled on the floor, giving me plenty of time to wonder why I'd suddenly taken us both into the deep end.

Because I wanted her to know, I decided. I didn't want her to have any doubts that I was interested, even if I couldn't do anything about it yet. I wanted her aware of me the way I was aware of her.

I wanted an answer to my question, too.

For a while, it didn't look as though I was going to get it. She seemed totally focused on the strip of wall she was painting next to the baseboard. At last, not looking up, she said, "I lived with a man for several years. His name was Steven. Steven Francis Blois."

I chewed over that for a moment, then offered, "There was a king of England named Stephen Blois. William the Conqueror's grandson."

She snorted. "Oh, yes. Every time Steven was introduced to someone he'd say, 'no relation.' When they looked confused or asked what he meant, he'd grin and add, 'to the former king of England, that is.'"

She bent and dipped her brush in the paint. "It was cute the first dozen or so times I heard it."

Sounded like she wasn't hung up on the man anymore. Encouraged, I said, "Stephen wasn't much of a king. Weak. The country was torn apart during his reign—barons chewing on other barons, eventually civil war."

"I don't think Steven knew or cared what kind of a king his namesake had been. He wasn't interested in history." She chuckled. "Actually, he was an accountant."

"An accountant." That sounded safe and dull. Of course, a builder might sound pretty dull, too. "Doesn't seem like your type."

"Do we have types?" She studied her handiwork, then shifted to touch up another section. "I thought he had an open, inquiring mind. He was very New Age, you see. Into meditation, drumming, psychic stuff."

Had he given her that chakra bracelet? I frowned. "Doesn't sound like any accountants I know."

"But he was still looking for rules, you see. Pigeonholes instead of answers. He didn't think outside the box—he just used a different set of boxes."

"So you're not still stuck on him?"

Now she looked up. "I told you about Steven because you asked why I'm not married. While we were together, I took that commitment very seriously. We were involved for six years, and lived together for five. But it ended with a fizzle, not a bang. That was over two years ago."

Steven Francis Blois must be a fool, to have had this woman for six years without marrying her. But maybe he'd wanted to get married. Maybe, for all her talk about taking the commitment seriously, she hadn't been interested in taking that last step. "So, was it you or him who thought living together was a good idea?"

Her lips twitched. "Something tells me you don't think much of living together without marriage."

"It isn't a moral thing for me. I just, ah…" Couldn't think of a tactful way to put it. Well, I'd warned her I was blunt. "It's always struck me as half-assed."

She didn't seem offended. "I take it you've never lived with anyone. What about marriage? Why have you never taken the plunge?"

"Uh…"

Her eyes lit with amusement. "Ben. You did open the subject for discussion, you know."

I guess I had, though that hadn't occurred to me when I blurted out my question. "I was serious about someone in college. Didn't work out. After that…well, for several years I was too blasted busy. Felt as if I had to set a good example—couldn't very well tell Charlie and Duncan how to act if I wasn't being responsible myself. And Annie. Lord." I shook my head. "I don't know how single parents do it. I didn't have time for much of a social life. Or the energy."

She made a listening sort of sound, and resumed painting. "Annie's the youngest, right? She's been an adult for a while now."

"I wasn't in a hurry to get tied down right away, once Annie went off to college. I guess I got out of the habit of thinking about marriage. It seemed like there was plenty of time."

"I imagine you were due a spell of blissful freedom. You'd been shortchanged on that when you were younger."

"By the time I started looking around…" I shrugged my good shoulder. "It's been suggested that I'm too picky."

She paused in her painting. Her eyes were serious when they met mine. The blue seemed darker, subdued, like a pond shadowed by trees, hiding what lay at the bottom. I wondered if she was thinking about Gwen and the child we shared. "And are you looking now? Is marriage what you want, Ben?"

"I'm forty years old."

She waited, letting her silence point out that I hadn't really answered the question.

I grimaced. I *had* opened the subject. "I want marriage, yeah. Kids to fill this old house with noise, skateboards, dolls, friends. Younger brothers or sisters to give their big brother a hard time. And a woman to share those kids with me." Someone who'd clutter the bathroom with female paraphernalia, and sleep beside me at night. Someone who would stay.

Her smile flashed, but somehow it seemed off. "Those skateboarding kids will turn into teenagers, you know. Your experience with your brothers and sisters didn't put you off?"

"It wasn't so bad. And maybe I learned a few things." I'd had about all the serious talk I could take. "What kind of teenager were you? Wild or studious? Not shy," I said definitely.

She chuckled and dipped her brush again. "Not studious, either. Though I wouldn't say I was wild, exactly—I couldn't bear to worry Daisy, so I didn't go too far. But I didn't have much sense. Is there anyone in the world as sure of themselves as eighteen-year-olds?"

We traded stories of our teenage days for a while. It looked as if she'd be able to finish up today, which wasn't bad for someone who'd never painted a room before. Of course, I'd helped a little. It didn't hurt my shoulder or my knee for me to sit on the floor and paint the strip next to the baseboards. Seely had argued some about that, but eventually she'd seen reason.

She was on the stepladder tackling the section next to the crown moldings by the time I figured out what was nagging at me.

Seely seemed open and outgoing. She swapped funny stories about growing up and spoke cheerfully about her eccentric mother. She'd told me about Steven, who I guess had been the one big love of her life.

But she'd never said which of them had preferred living together to marriage. She hadn't said anything about why she'd moved out, either, just that it happened two years ago. Yesterday she'd admitted to being angry with her father, but hadn't told me the man's name, or anything else about him. And she'd implied that anything weird I'd seen that night on the mountain must have been the product of shock.

Slippery.

Seely Jones was a much more private woman than she seemed. I could respect that, and yet…I glanced uneasily at the unopened box beside the couch.

Last year I'd gone wireless when I got a new laptop. It didn't have to be hooked up to anything to connect to the Internet. So, on my first night home from the hospital I'd ordered several books on-line, paying to have them overnighted. I probably could have gotten them, or something similar, from the bookstore on Fremont Street. Susannah would have boxed up my order and dropped them off, if I'd asked.

Or I could have gotten books from the library for nothing. I'd known the head librarian since I was five. Muriel would have looked up my card number, checked the books out to me and brought them by.

But anyone who knew me would have been startled by my current choice of reading material. I didn't want to explain. I didn't want anyone speculating about my sanity, either. I was doing enough of that.

Finding myself in the company of Harold Meckle, M.D., was a nasty shock, but like I said, he wasn't really an idiot. Just a jerk. Some of the things that happened on that mountain didn't add up, not using any of the normal ways of calculating reality.

"That bracelet you wear," I mentioned as I finished the last bit I could reach. "Did Blois give it to you?"

She didn't turn around. "Why do you ask?"

"You said the little stones were for, uh, chakras. And that Blois was into New Age stuff."

"Daisy gave it to me—her version of a 'sweet sixteen' present."

"She's into chakras?"

"Among other things."

I decided not to press for more. Not now. I'd gotten one solid answer—Blois hadn't given her the bracelet she never seemed to remove. That was something. Far from all I needed to know, though. Maybe I'm too stubborn for my own good. I've been told that more than once.

I wondered what Duncan would say about the request I planned to make the next time I saw him.

Seven

"Look, if you don't want to do it, just say so."

"I don't want to do it."

I sighed.

Duncan and I were sitting at the kitchen table with some of Seely's excellent coffee. She was upstairs getting ready.

Not that she needed to. We were just going to drop by the office—though I hadn't mentioned that part yet—then head to the building-supply center. And she already looked great. She always did.

But women have rules for that sort of thing. Not the same rules, mind—they vary from one woman to the next in some sort of changeable code. It seems to make sense to other women.

Setting has something to do with it. When Annie was doing handyman work, she'd run all over town in paint-splattered jeans or coveralls, her face bare of makeup and her hair tucked

up in a cap. Dealing with clients or stopping at the gas station dressed that way was okay; going to the grocery store was
not. I know this because she used to kick up a fuss if I asked
her to pick up something while she was out. "I can't go to the
grocery store looking like this!" she'd say, even though plenty
of people had seen her looking like that already.

Apparently, building-supply centers belonged in the "get
fixed up first" category for Seely. I didn't try to understand it.

I collected my walking stick and mug and lifted my left
foot off the extra chair. My knee was a lot better, but I still
kept that leg propped up much of the time. I limped over to
the coffeepot. "Want some more?"

Duncan shook his head. He was looking tired, I thought.
Night shifts didn't agree with him. Then, too, he'd pulled a
double in order to free up time for the camping trip with
Zach—a trip the weather had cut short. We'd had our first
good freeze Saturday night, accompanied by a light dusting
of snow.

Duncan's gaze held steady on me as I refilled my mug.
"Maybe you should tell me why you asked. If you suspect
Seely has a criminal background—"

"Nothing like that," I said quickly. "There's something
she's not telling me, that's all."

His mouth crooked up. "More than one thing, probably.
Women have been failing to tell men everything for a few
thousand years. Police departments don't generally consider
that a good reason to run a background check."

He made my curiosity sound like a man-woman thing, not
employer-employee. Which was accurate but annoying. "I
didn't want you to do it as a cop."

"Well, as your brother I'm advising you to drop the idea."
He put the mug down. "Nosing around will just get you in

trouble. Though if you really have to know something, you could hire a P.I."

No way. I'd thought maybe Duncan could find out a few things discreetly. Her father's name, for example. Some hint of why she was working at jobs way below her skill level. But I didn't want some stranger snooping around in her life. "Never mind."

"You know, this is weird."

"What?"

"You. You're acting different." He nodded toward the front of the house. "The living room. It's always been white."

"You don't like it green?"

"It looks fine. Felt weird when I walked in and saw it, though." One corner of his mouth kicked up, as if he were reluctantly amused. "Sort of like a kid who goes away to college, comes home and finds out mom and dad redecorated without telling him."

Dammit, I should have thought about how he'd feel. Charlie and Annie, too. This house was their heritage every bit as much as it was mine. "I ought to have said something. It's your house, too, and you—"

"No, it isn't."

"Of course it is. Mom and Dad left it to all of us."

"Twenty years ago, yes. But you're the one who has lived here all these years, taken care of the place. This is your home." He took a deep breath. "Gwen and I have talked about this. We want to deed my share of the house over to you."

I slammed my mug down, ignoring the coffee that slopped over the rim. "Forget it."

"There might be some tax liability for you, but she thinks we can minimize that."

"Aren't you listening?" I demanded. "Just because your wife could buy and sell this house ten times over doesn't oblige me to accept a handout."

Duncan shoved to his feet. "This has nothing to do with Gwen's money! Dammit, you hard-headed son of a bitch, will you listen a minute?"

"I'm not hearing anything worth listening to. If you don't—"

"Whoa!"

That came from Seely. Startled, I looked at the doorway.

She stood there, shaking her head. "Good grief. I can't be accused of eavesdropping with Ben bellowing like a wounded moose. I heard him from the stairs. Ben." She fixed me with a firm stare. "Do you really think Duncan offered to give you his share of this house because he enjoys flinging Gwen's money around?"

I flushed. "No. But—"

"Not your turn." She sauntered on into the kitchen, stopping in front of Duncan. "And did you really think Ben would take your inheritance from you?"

"That's not what this is about."

"It is to him." She put her hands on her hips and looked from one to the other of us. "This is none of my business, of course. But it seems pretty simple. Ben lives here. Duncan doesn't. Ben, I don't know how you're fixed financially, but could you buy Duncan's share?"

"Sure." I turned some numbers over in my head. The business had done well the past few years, and I wasn't exactly extravagant. "We'll need to get the place appraised, but I've got a pretty good idea of its current market value."

Duncan shook his head. "We don't want to use the current market value. It's worth three times what it was twenty years ago, and none of us are going to make a profit off you. Charlie suggested—"

"You talked to Charlie about this? What is this, some kind of conspiracy?"

"Exactly. Annie, too. The plan was to wait until we could all be home at the same time and tackle you together. I, uh, jumped the gun."

Seely chuckled. "Safety in numbers. A legitimate military tactic."

I glanced at her. Did she know that Duncan had been in the Army until a few months ago? Probably. If Duncan hadn't mentioned it, Gwen would have. People told her things.

"If you're all in this together," I told my brother, "you need to drop this notion of giving up your shares in the house for little or nothing. Charlie won't take a fair price for his share if you and Annie don't. The two of you may not need the money, but he does." He'd just sunk every cent he had or could borrow into a partnership in a landscaping business. I'd already tried to give him a loan. Twice.

Duncan frowned. I decided to let him chew on that a while and turned to Seely. "Looks like you're ready to go."

She looked a damned sight better than "ready to go." All that gorgeous hair spilled over her shoulders and down her back, and I could tell she'd fussed with makeup, turning her eyes sultry and her lips scarlet. She wore dark jeans and a sweater with geometric shapes in red, purple and yellow.

That sweater fit more snugly than anything I'd seen her wear before. My body took notice of this. Of course, my body had been on yellow alert almost constantly for the past three days.

"Just let me get my jacket and purse," she said, and headed for the hall.

"I'd better be going, too," Duncan said, carrying his mug

over to the sink. "What are you getting at the building supply store?"

"We're going to put up some shelves in my office here."

"I take it the 'we' means you're supervising?"

"All right, *she's* going to put them up. I'm not taking advantage of her. She's keen on all this home fixup and decorating stuff."

"Hmm." He stuck his mug in the dishwasher. "I owe Seely a thank-you."

"I'll tell her you enjoyed the coffee."

He slanted me an amused glance. "I didn't mean for the coffee."

It felt weird to sit in the passenger seat of my own car.

The Chevy was backup transportation, nearly ten years old but in good shape. Power windows, doors and steering; bench seats and a big back seat…big enough to give me some impractical ideas. Sexual frustration was bringing out the adolescent in me.

Seely drove with the same unrushed efficiency she did everything else. "I still don't know how I let you talk me into taking you by the office. You aren't supposed to be working yet."

I pointed out that I hadn't worked—I'd just checked on the work others were doing. I hadn't even insisted on going to the Pearson site.

She grinned. "I suppose you think you get Brownie points for that."

"I ought to." If sexual frustration was robbing her of sleep and nudging stupid ideas into her head, it didn't show.

"You're staring at me."

"I like looking at you."

The faintest flush mounted her cheeks. Maybe I shouldn't

have said anything. I'd been careful not to since letting her know my intentions. That was the right thing to do. Sexual innuendos were out of place while she was working for me. Besides, self-preservation called for restraint. I had to keep my eye on the line I'd drawn, or I'd find myself tumbling off another edge.

But I liked seeing that flush.

I'd spent too much time the past three days trying to figure out what was going on in her head. We had something strong and hot flowing between us. I knew that much because I'd caught her looking at me a few times, too. At twenty, I'd have assumed that meant she agreed with me, that she wanted to have an affair as soon as the employer-employee thing was out of the way.

At forty, I knew better.

At least she hadn't told me to forget it. I figured she was still making up her mind about me. I didn't say anything else until she'd shut off the engine, hoping she'd spend the time thinking about the heat between us.

I pushed open my door. "You sure you want to tackle this? Putting up shelves isn't easy. Goes a lot better with two people, and I won't be able to help much."

"You won't be helping at all," she retorted, coming around the car.

I made a noncommittal noise. No point in mentioning that there would be parts of the job where two pairs of hands would be necessary.

She matched her pace to mine—which was slow. I didn't limp anymore as long as I didn't try to outrace a snail. "This is my chance to learn from an expert," she said. "I'm not about to pass that up."

"Well, the expert suggests we get red oak. It's not easy to

work with, but it should look great." I paused, considering the state of my office. "Eventually."

"It is a bit of a mess in there."

I grunted. The doors opened for us and I crept along to the left, where the lumber was stacked. I'd pick out the wood myself, that being the reason for this trip. Well, that and a bad case of cabin fever. We wouldn't be able to take it home today, obviously, since I didn't have a truck.

And we wouldn't be able to do much with the wood until we'd cleared the place out. The room I used for a home office used to be a bedroom—my parents' bedroom, actually. I'd taken their bed out about a month after they died, unable to stand seeing it there, all made up and waiting for them. Eventually Annie had claimed their dresser. Somehow I'd never gotten around to clearing everything else out, though.

My two favorite spots in the store were the tool aisles and the lumber section. Tools are always interesting, and being surrounded by all that wood hits me viscerally. I think it's the smell—cut wood, sawdust, a whiff of sap.

Ed noticed my sling and the walking stick, so of course he had to hear the whole story, then felt obligated to spend some time assuring me I was lucky to be alive before he could put my order together. I arranged to have it picked up in a couple days. "That will give me a chance to clear the room out," I told Seely as we headed for the front of the store with the ticket. Our slow speed wasn't just due to my pace this time—she kept stopping to look at paint chips and light fixtures.

"Us," she said. "It's not as if I have much else to do. And we don't have to remove everything. You have some good pieces in there, like that occasional table with the Queen Anne legs."

"Yeah?" I smiled, pleased. "I made that when I was sixteen."

"You're kidding!"

"Shop class. It was a Christmas gift for my mom. I was trying to copy a picture I found in a magazine. Put in a lot of extra hours on it…had a lot of help, too." As I spoke I saw Mr. Nelson's face. He'd been the soul of patience, often staying late so I could work in the shop. "Lord, I hadn't thought of Mr. Nelson in years."

"Your teacher?"

"Yeah. He retired while I was away at college, moved to Albuquerque to be near his sister. He was an old bachelor, you see. I stopped in to see him once when I was there on business…" My voice trailed away as I remembered that visit. How sorry I'd felt for the old man, living alone, no one but a sister nearby. All of a sudden I could see my own future, and it didn't look much different.

I had Zach, I reminded myself. Some of the time, at least.

"What's the matter?"

"Nothing." We'd reached the front of the store. I headed for the nearest checkout. "I'm amazed that you let me get up here without buying anything else. Why is someone who calls herself a wanderer so interested in everything to do with houses?"

She shrugged. "The fascination of the exotic, perhaps. I've never rooted anywhere long enough to do much in the way of home improvement, so it seems novel and exciting. Does your interest in construction go back to that woodworking class?"

"Partly. Do you do that on purpose?"

"What?"

"Turn the conversation away from yourself and back on me. Annie tells me that all a woman has to do to appear fascinating to a man is to get him to talk about himself. Maybe that's true. But I'd like to hear about you sometimes."

A flush climbed the crest of her cheekbones. She gave me

a teasing smile. "Does that mean it's working? You think I'm
fascinating?"

I'd have enjoyed her flirting a lot more if I hadn't thought
she was using it to duck the question. "Look, I don't know—
what is it?"

She'd gone dead pale. She was staring over my shoulder.
I turned.

Someone was staring back. An old woman, every inch as
tall as Seely but skinnier, like a dried-out string bean, had
stopped a few feet away. She had a real lost-in-the-fifties look
going, right down to the low heels and pearls. Her coat was
dark-blue wool. Her gray hair had been permed, teased and
sprayed into submission.

And her expression was venomous. "You! What are you
doing here?"

"Buying lumber." Seely's voice was steady. Her face was
blank and much too pale. "Why? What are you doing here?"

"Don't you smart off to me! You're not supposed to be
here! You said you were leaving. You don't belong here. We
don't want you here. Don't think you'll get a penny from me,
whatever tricks you pull!"

"I don't want your money. I never did." Seely started to
turn away.

"Nasty baggage! You'll listen when I talk to you." The
woman started after her. "I won't have you confusing John,
making him miserable again—"

"Mrs. Lake," I said loudly. "Do you realize how worried
your daughter has been?"

She jolted. I don't think she'd noticed me until that second,
which says a lot about how focused she'd been on Seely. I'm
not easy to overlook. Faded-blue eyes blinked behind her bi-
focals. "What? I'm not—"

"I know," I said soothingly, and switched my walking stick to my right hand so I could take her arm. My shoulder twinged. "Not yourself these days, are you? But if you'd take your medication you'd feel better. You have to stop wandering off this way. Poor Melly is frantic."

She stared up at me as if I were mad. "If you don't take your hand off me this instant I will have you arrested."

I leaned closer and muttered, "You've drawn quite a crowd. Maybe you like scenes. If so, go right ahead and screech some more."

She looked around. People were staring, all right. The clerk had stopped ringing up her customer.

Color flooded the old woman's scrawny neck.

Seely spoke from behind me. "I can handle this, Ben."

"So? You don't have to."

The old woman drew herself up. "You'll be sorry you interfered. I'll tell the judge, and he'll see to it. As for *you*…" She leaned around me, her eyes glittered with malice. "Devil child! You stay away from me and mine."

She jerked her arm out of my grip and turned away with surprising dignity. I watched just long enough to make sure that she was really leaving, then looked at Seely.

Her lips were tight. There was a lost look about her eyes I didn't like. "I'm sorry. I didn't know…I didn't expect to see her at a place like this. I wouldn't have subjected you to that scene if I'd had any idea she might…" Her throat worked as she swallowed.

"Yeah, I'm all torn up about it." I gripped her elbow and started for the doors. "Come on."

"But—the wood! You can't…Ben?"

"Give her the ticket." I nodded at the clerk as we passed the checkout. The others in the line glared at me. "McClain

Construction," I told the clerk. "Charge it, save it, toss it, whatever. I'll call."

We went through the automatic doors at a better pace than I'd managed since falling off the mountain. No doubt my knee would complain later. I didn't care. Seely needed to get out, away from all those curious eyes.

She didn't mention my knee or my shoulder, either out loud or with her eyebrows. Which just confirmed how upset she was. She did say something about me being high-handed.

"You need to scream, cry or throw things. You don't want to do that here, so we're going home."

"I am not going to cry."

"Yeah, I figured you were more a thrower than a crier. Here we are." I released her arm and opened the passenger door.

"Wait a minute. I'm driving."

"No, you aren't." I headed around the front of the car. "Power steering, power brakes and my right leg and left arm work fine. I don't know why I let you talk me into the passenger seat in the first place."

"I've got the keys. You are not driving, Ben."

"You've got a set of keys." I used the ones in my hand to open my door, tossed my walking stick in the back seat, and lowered myself carefully behind the wheel. Damn. I'd been right about my knee. "You coming?"

She came. She slammed the door, but she came.

Eight

Seely didn't say a thing for several blocks, just sat there hugging her elbows tight to her body, as if they might get away from her otherwise.

Making her mad hadn't worked, except as a temporary fix. She'd fallen right back into whatever unhappy thoughts held her prisoner. I was hunting for another strategy when she broke the silence. "What was that bit about Melly?"

"I made that up. Got the old biddy's attention."

"It did do that," she said dryly.

"So who is she? Looked like someone freeze-dried June Cleaver's mother."

Her laugh broke out. Out of the corner of my eye I saw her arms loosen. "Don't surprise me like that! I nearly choked. Her name is Helen Burns. Mrs. Randall Burns, to be precise."

"Who's the judge she threatened me with?"

"Her husband. Who hasn't sat on the bench in twenty years, but she isn't about to let anyone forget that he used to."

"Hmm." I'd heard of the judge, of course. Didn't think I'd ever met the man.

I turned onto Oak. My street was one of the oldest in town, more level than recent construction, which has to crowd its way up the slopes that cradle Highpoint. The houses here have a settled look; some are large, some smaller, but all have good-size yards. For a short stretch, trees from both sides of the road clasped hands over the street.

We emerged from the tree tunnel onto my block. Smoke puffed from the Berringtons' chimney. Jack Robert's truck was in the driveway. Looked like he still hadn't found another position after being laid off two months ago. The Frasers were out front, old Walt cleaning out a gutter while Shirley steadied the ladder.

I knew the houses along here, the changes that had been made in and around them over the years, the names, stories and people who belonged to those houses. Some people don't like seeing the same faces and places all the time. Take my brother Charlie. He drove a truck for years because he liked staying on the move, always seeing something new. And I'm not sure Annie's husband, Jack, will ever settle permanently in one place.

That's hard for a rooted man like me to understand. Did the world's wanderers have any idea what they were missing? Or were they so busy chasing the horizon they never realized what they'd given up?

I pulled into my driveway, cut the engine and glanced at the woman beside me...one of the wanderers. I shook my head. "If you're keeping quiet in the hope that I'll be too tactful to ask why Mrs. Randall Burns hates your guts, you're out of luck."

She snorted. "I'm not such a blind optimist. Anyway,

you're due an explanation." She looked down, plucking at a snag near the hem of her sweater. "Helen Burns hates me for being born. Bad blood, you see. She's my grandmother."

I closed my mouth before any more stupid comments could escape. "Inside. We'll talk about it inside."

She didn't quite slam the door when she got out. "There's nothing to talk about."

That remark was obviously the product of wishful thinking. "I take it she's your father's mother. The father you don't know anything about."

"When I told you that I was trying to preserve a little privacy. Not a concept you have a lot of respect for…oh, do slow down, Ben. You're obviously hurting."

"I'm okay. So does he live here, too? Here in Highpoint?"

"Yes." She didn't wait for me to obey—or not—but moved up beside me and slid her arm around my waist, forcing me to move slower. "And yes, that's why I came to Highpoint—sheer, bloody-minded curiosity."

A quick jolt of heat distracted me…and a quieter warmth seeped inside, unknotting muscles I hadn't realized were clenched. The pain in my shoulder eased to a dull ache.

I frowned at the top of her head. She was looking down, as if the stairs to the porch required a lot of attention. "You wanted to meet him?"

"No. There may be a touch of masochist in me, but I don't let it take over. I wanted to see him, find out about him, that's all."

We'd reached the door. I let her use her key while I tried to sort out the difference between one kind of heat and another. "Wanting to know your father isn't masochistic."

"No? And yet you've met his mother." She swung the door open.

I limped inside. "How did she recognize you, if you haven't had any contact all these years?"

"My mother sent my father school pictures and little notes every year. I suppose he might have shown them to Granny Dearest. Or maybe she recognized me from the last time we met, twenty-four years ago." She slapped her purse down on the hall table. "Does it matter?"

Twenty-four years ago... "When you were eight? That was the last time you saw your father, you said. That was when you last saw your grandmother, too?"

"Daisy hit a hard patch financially that summer. Things were always tight, but then she had her purse snatched and there went the rent money. My father..." Her voice faltered. "He'd been gone three years by then, but hadn't yet dropped out of my life completely. She called him, asked for help."

"Did you go stay with him?"

"Not exactly. He was working toward his master's and didn't have a penny to spare. So he said, anyway. I wound up being shipped up here to stay with the judge and my grandmother. My father drove up on weekends, or sometimes we drove into Denver to see him."

"You didn't get along with your grandparents."

"That's putting it mildly." She shrugged out of her jacket and opened the hall closet. "Can we drop the subject now?"

"In a minute. Your grandmother knew you were in town. She claimed you'd told her you were leaving."

"She and the judge ate at the lodge one night. I waited on their table." She grimaced. "Not a happy encounter for any of us."

"Why didn't you—"

"Ben! Stop interrogating me. You need to sit down, get off your knee."

I didn't want to sit. I couldn't pace very well, dammit, but

I sure didn't want to sit. "If I don't ask questions, you won't tell me anything."

"Why should I?"

"Why shouldn't you? Lord, I never knew a woman so good at turning away questions! If I ask a single personal question, I end up talking about my own father. Or the best color for the hall bath, or how to repair damaged plaster."

Anger waved flags in her cheeks. "You're exaggerating." She spun and headed for the living room.

"Am I?" I hobbled after her. "You led me to think you didn't know anything about your father's side of the family. If we hadn't run into your old witch of a grandmother—"

Her laugh was short, sharp and ugly. "Oh, but she's not the witch. That's the problem. My other grandmother is. Literally."

God help me. I leaned my stick carefully against the wall. "Your mother's mother is, uh…"

"A witch." Mockery gleamed in her eyes.

"Okay." I nodded slowly. "I got that part. You mean like Wicca and all that?"

"That's what people call it nowadays. Granny doesn't, and really, I'm not sure how much a New Age witch would have in common with Granny's brand of the Craft."

She believed this. She honestly thought her grandmother was a witch. "And do you think…uh, are you one, too?"

"The word is witch, Ben. And no, I'm not. But I'm the granddaughter of one, which makes me Satan's get in the eyes of Mrs. Randall Burns. Didn't you hear the part about me being a devil child?"

"Somehow that didn't immediately bring witchcraft to mind." Muddy floors, yes. Witchcraft, no.

"I suppose not. Will you get off that damned knee?"

"I don't think I've heard you curse before," I observed.

"You could make a saint curse!"

"I'll sit down if you'll tell me about your grandmother. Your *other* grandmother, not the one I just met."

She muttered something unflattering about my antecedents, then flung up her hands. "Okay. Her name is Alma Jones. She's eighty-four and the top of her head barely reaches my shoulder. She lives…*sit,* Ben!"

"I'm sitting." I lowered myself onto the couch.

"She lives in a tiny cottage in the Appalachians and makes the world's best chicken and dumplings. Fresh chicken, mind, from her henhouse. She also makes simples, little charms and cures to sell to her neighbors, and she has the Sight."

"Ah…the Sight. That's a Celtic thing, isn't it? Irish or Scottish?"

"Her maiden name was Sullivan." The laid-back woman I'd known for a week fairly bristled with feeling. Even her hair seemed agitated. She began pacing. "She's a darling. She's helped people all her life. She didn't ask to have the Sight. Who would? But it runs in our family. Like the curse."

The curse?

Seely reached the end of the room and spun around, making her hair fly out like a curly cape. "Do you know what that self-righteous old prune called her? A bride of Satan. My granny! She taught Sunday school for thirty-two years!"

A Christian witch. Well, if you could believe in witchcraft in the first place, why not? "What curse?"

She grimaced. "I didn't mean to mention that."

"Too late now. What curse?"

"The one another witch put on my great-grandmother for stealing her man about a hundred years ago." She flung up her hands. "Why am I telling you all this? You don't believe a word of it."

"I believe several parts," I said cautiously. Her granny probably was a good, loving woman who'd taught Sunday school and made up little herbal remedies for her neighbors. And thought of herself as a witch.

Seely's expression softened as the corners of her lips turned up. "Poor Ben. You're trying so hard not to tell me that I'm nuts. If it's any consolation, I don't believe in the curse, either."

"Okay. The curse doesn't count. But you said it was passed down in your family like, uh, the Sight."

"I've heard about it all my life. I don't really believe in it, but…" She shrugged, which gave her breasts a gentle lift.

I wanted to tell her how much I liked that sweater. I didn't even let my gaze linger, an act of willpower for which I deserved a lot more credit than I was likely to get. "I know how family stories stick with you. We learn things when we're kids that cling like burrs long after we've figured out they aren't really true."

"Yes!" Her laugh was shaky. "That's it exactly. I don't really believe in the curse, yet I can't completely forget it, either. Daisy believes it." Her feet started her moving again. "She thinks my father left us because a witch cursed the women in my family to unhappiness in love."

"Hmm."

She paused by the window, shrugged. "I guess it's easier to believe in a curse than to think that he didn't really love her. Or that he's a noodle."

"Cooked, I take it."

She nodded and ran her fingers along the edge of the drapes, as if she found it easier to talk to them right now, instead of me. "I made it sound like I don't remember anything about him. That isn't quite true. He read me bedtime stories. He used to take me out in this little sidecar attached to his bicycle. I remember the way the fields smelled, the tug of the wind in my hair." She swallowed. "The sound of his laugh.'"

"Sounds like a noodle, all right." I came up behind her and rested my hand on her shoulder. "He loved you. For some reason he wasn't man enough to be responsible for you, but he loved you."

"You aren't on the couch."

"Nope." I folded my good arm around her and eased her up against me.

She didn't exactly resist, but she didn't relax, either. "Ben…'

I had a hunch she'd like it better if I made a pass. She'd know what to do when a man crossed that kind of boundary. Comfort was harder for her.

Tough. I stroked a hand down her hair. "So what's the noodle's name? Burns for the last half, I guess. Zebediah? Ezekiel?"

My hand was resting against the side of her face, so I felt her smile even though I couldn't see it. "Well, it is biblical.'

"Mathew? Mark?" She'd relaxed against me, slightly sideways because of the sling. Her hip nestled into my groin. I wondered how long my brain could survive without oxygen, seeing that all of my blood was tied up in one part of my body. "Do I need to run through the rest of the Gospels?"

Her low chuckle delighted me. "Old Testament. Think lions."

"Lion's den. Daniel."

"Bingo." The top of her head was even with my eyes. Her hair was so soft…. I didn't nuzzle it. Surely some celestial scorekeeper was pasting all kinds of gold stars next to my name. "I'm glad Duncan turned me down. Better to hear all this from you."

She went stiff. "What do you mean, he turned you down?"

Uh-oh. Too much distraction. "Let's pretend I didn't say that."

"Oh, no." She turned, pulling out of my arms, a dangerous glint in her eyes. "I want to know what you meant."

"You weren't telling me things. Important things. So I...hell." I ran my hand over my own head this time.

"So you had me checked out? You had your brother check me out?"

"No, I told you—he turned me down."

"Oh, that's different, then! You *wanted* the cops to investigate me, but your brother wouldn't do it, so everything's fine!"

"I needed to know about you, okay? I didn't want to know. I *needed* to. And if that doesn't make sense, well, tough. Tough on both of us," I said, my voice getting louder, "because I'm *used* to making sense, only here you are, and I keep doing *stupid* things and I don't know why! I don't make sense at all anymore!"

For a second after my outburst, there was silence. I scowled at her. She was smiling, dammit. "And you like that."

Her smile just got wider. Then she lifted up onto her toes, put her hand on my good shoulder and her mouth right smack on mine.

"You..." Hard to form words with my head buzzing this way. "Why did you do that?"

"Impulse." She skimmed smiling lips across mine. "Very poor impulse control I have at times."

I, on the other hand, was great at self-control. I proved it by not grabbing her.

"Oh, dear, here comes another one. Help," she said, sliding her arms around my neck and tickling my nape with her fingers. "They're coming pretty fast now. Can't seem to stop them."

"Stop..." Her body brushed mine, scattering what passed for my thoughts. "Stop what?"

"Impulses. Wicked ones. Whoops." She slipped the top button of my shirt from its buttonhole. "See what I mean?"

"Ah…" I ran my fingers down the whole, wiggly length of her hair, then slowly wrapped my hand around a hunk of it. "This sort of thing, you mean?" And I bent my head and licked her bottom lip. "I'm not supposed to do that."

"Exactly." That word glided out on a puff of breath. "I guess they're catching."

Another button met the fate of the first. And I snapped.

My left arm clamped around her waist—and damn that sling! I couldn't snug her against me the way I wanted. But I could crush my mouth down on hers. I could catch her sigh as her lips parted and send my tongue to steal her taste, take it inside me.

I needed two hands. Hell, I could have used three or four, there were so many places I wanted to touch, but I made do with what was available. She'd fitted herself up against me as closely as possible, so I turned my left hand loose to wander.

It liked the taut shape of her thigh, the flare of her hip, the muscle and flesh of her bottom…but that sweater. I'd been looking at that sweater all day, imagining what lay beneath it. I nudged her legs apart with my knee, making a space for my leg between hers. And slid my hand up under her sweater.

"Lace," I groaned as my hand found the warmth and weight of her breast. "This damned sweater made me crazy enough. If I'd known there was lace beneath it…" I rubbed her nipple with my thumb and pressed up with my thigh.

She moaned into my mouth. Then bit my lip.

"I want this." I squeezed her nipple between my thumb and forefinger. "I want to see this."

The shiver that rippled up her spine struck me as agreement, but she shook her head as she slid one hand up my chest. "I'd have to let go of you to take it off. And I don't want to."

That was a problem, all right. I admit I wasn't much help, since I claimed her mouth again when she scraped my nipple with a fingernail. Her mouth was warm and sweet and a little wild, and though something was nagging at the back of my brain, telling me to slow down and think, I wasn't listening.

Vertical was losing all appeal. I wanted to be horizontal, where the lack of one hand wouldn't matter so much.

I also wanted her naked. "Damn," I muttered against the column of her neck as that vagrant thought finally surfaced. Reluctantly I eased away. "Hold on. We're by the window, and the drapes are open."

"Oh. I forgot. I can't believe…" She laughed unsteadily and pushed her hair back from her face with both hands. "Good grief. I'm glad you thought of it."

"Yeah." When I pulled the drapes closed, the light dimmed and softened. I smiled. "Now you can take that sweater off."

"Um…there's something I should say first."

"If you've changed your mind…" I grabbed for self-control. Never had it felt more slippery. "I won't yell. I might whimper a bit or beg. But I won't yell."

"No. Oh, no." She wrapped her arms around my waist and leaned into me. "I just wanted to make sure we're on the same page. I can't picture myself staying in Highpoint, exchanging friendly greetings with my grandmother in the produce section. And I can't picture you anywhere else."

Some emotion landed with a jolt in my stomach. "So you're saying we should have fun, but nothing serious."

"Something like that."

She'd stolen my lines, dammit. The warning I was supposed to give her. The conditions I'd forgotten about. The ones I wasn't sure I wanted anymore.

This wasn't the time to mention that. I bent and nuzzled

her hair away from her ear so I could kiss her there. "I never argue with a lady who's about to remove her sweater."

Her chuckle sounded relieved. "You've got a thing about my sweater."

"Oh, yeah. I'd do it myself if I could." I longed to strip her slowly, teasing and touching and kissing as I went. I couldn't even undress myself properly, dammit.

Which left me supervising again. I ran my tongue along the cord of her neck, then released her and waved my hand. "Up and off."

"Bossy," she observed, but her voice was husky. She grasped the hem on her sweater, peeling it up over her head.

Lace. Her breasts were cupped in it, full half-moons of creamy flesh overlaid with white lace, with darker nipples and areolas peeking through. Her hair spilled over bare shoulders, one curly strand falling in a soft hook around one dark-tipped breast.

My mouth went dry and my heart tried to hammer its way out of my chest. "Did I mention that lace makes me crazy? Never mind," I said, forgetting my plan to get horizontal. I brushed the skin above the lacy edge of her bra. "I'll show you."

"Wait a minute," she said, and stepped back a couple of paces.

Something in her voice brought my gaze to her face. Her smile was the same, that easy curve of lips. But nerves or uncertainty jumped in her eyes. I wanted to wrap her close in my arms—hell, my one good arm—and soothe her. I took a step forward.

"Uh-uh." She tossed her hair back, lifted one eyebrow. "You're not in charge here, bud."

I wasn't?

"Wait," she ordered. Her hands went to the waist of her jeans. I'm no fool. I waited.

She stripped for me. First she unfastened the jeans, giving me a peek beneath while she toed off her shoes. Then the socks, and how anyone could turn the removal of socks into a tease I don't know, but she did. Then she shoved the jeans down and stepped out of them.

A slim dip of a waist, and more lace below—white again, riding low on her hips, darker at the notch of her legs. "You have the most magnificent legs I've ever seen."

She blinked once, like a surprised cat. "Well. And here I thought it was my breasts you were fixated on." She reached behind her with both hands, which lifted her breasts in a way that nearly made me swallow my tongue. And unfastened her bra.

Magnificent was too pale a word. But when I went to her, I put my hand in the center of her chest, not over one of those bare, perfect breasts. I looked at her face. "Your heart's pounding."

She lifted one eyebrow. "I'm excited."

Her voice, her posture, that coolly lifted eyebrow—all spoke of confidence and experience. She knew her body could make a man beg. But while passion might ripen the heart's rhythm, it didn't send it tripping this fast, this hard, as if it were trying to flee. Not unless some other feelings were mixed in.

I didn't tell her I didn't believe her. I didn't follow the instinct that demanded I gather her close, stroking her back until whatever fears rode her had eased. Naked bodies didn't bother Seely. Tenderness would.

The time would come when I wanted her feelings as naked as the rest of her, but not yet. Not today. I touched her cheek and promised silently I would treasure and protect whatever she shared with me. Her body, for now.

Her eyes closed. "You are a devious man," she whispered.

I nodded. Then, at last, I cupped her breast. "You feel like rose petals." I stroked, cupped and lifted, then bent to take the hard little pebble of her nipple in my mouth.

Her breath sucked in. Her fingers fretted my hair, skimmed my jaw as I switched breasts. She made a pleased sound, then, after a moment, said, "As your medical attendant, I insist that you get off your feet. Quickly."

I licked her nipple, then blew on it. "Want to play doctor, do you?"

"Yes." She threaded her fingers through my hair, pulled my head up and kissed me. "And the doctor will see you now." Her hands went to the snap on my jeans. "All of you."

Nine

Seely believed in giving a thorough examination. And she was right—I wasn't in charge. Or in control in anyway; not for long.

The couch was warm and soft against my bare back and butt. The woman on top of me was softer and a lot warmer.

She also possessed a mean streak I hadn't suspected.

"No more," I said, then groaned as she immediately disobeyed, drawing her fingernail along the taut skin behind my balls. "Vicious," I observed when I got some breath back.

She was on her hands and knees over me. Her breasts rose and fell rapidly and her hair hung down, tickling my chest. Her lips were shiny and damp, curved in a feline smile.

It wasn't my mouth she'd been kissing. "I haven't completed my tests," she informed me. "That swelling you're experiencing is quite remarkable. Bears further study." She started to scoot back down my body.

I growled, looped a hank of her hair around my hand and tugged. "C'mere, woman."

She came, stretching out all along me. "*Tch.* You aren't supposed to grab the doctor by the hair."

"No respect for authority. That's my problem." I urged her head close enough for a kiss. While I made my point with my tongue, I nudged my hips up. The way she was straddling me left her wide open. I rubbed the head of my penis along her slick folds.

She gasped. Her eyes opened wide. "Vicious."

"Payback's a bitch," I agreed. I teased both of us until I couldn't play anymore. Not in any way. "Seely. Now. Let it be now. I need you."

She looked as if I'd said that one of us only had a week left to live. "Don't."

"Too late." I kissed that stricken look off her face, gripped her hip to hold her in place and slid inside.

She moaned. Pleasure swirled, a tactile kaleidoscope spiraling up from my groin to surround me, body, brain and soul. Her nails dug into my shoulder, a prick of pain that all but sent me over the edge. I hung on, not daring to move.

A thought floated up.

I moaned again, but not with pleasure. "I forgot. I can't believe I forgot."

"Hmm?" Her eyelids were at half-mast, her face flushed. "I don't think you've forgotten anything." She wiggled. "Yep, everything's in place, which is a wonder. I was not entirely sure you'd fit."

"I'm naked." I fought the need to move. "*Completely* naked."

"I don't...oh." Something other than passion flitted through her eyes. "Not a problem. I can't get pregnant or catch anything from you. Or give anything to you, for that matter."

Being on the pill didn't protect her from STDs. Seely wasn't stupid—she had to know that. I opened my mouth to say so, but she bent and captured it, and I lost track of words.

I did manage a weak protest after a moment, something about protecting her.

"Shh. It's all right, Ben. You can let go. This once, you don't have to be responsible. It will be okay. I promise."

It couldn't have been what she said, because that didn't make sense. Maybe it was the way she touched my face—gently, as if I were the fragile one. Or the way her hips moved, taking me in, all the way in, then rising slowly to do it again. Or the way she moaned, as if—in this one way, at least—she needed me, too.

Or maybe I lost it, all by myself. Whatever the reason, something inside me snapped. I began pumping up into her. Seely moaned, threw her head back and rode me clear to paradise.

I lay on my left side, watching Seely sleep. Her hair was all over the place. I wanted to play with it, but my only usable arm was propping me up so I could look at her. And I didn't want to stop looking.

She was cuddled up against me, her breathing soft and even. The twin fans of her eyelashes spread in tidy symmetry along the tender skin beneath her eyes. The room was murky with early twilight, as if a storm was moving in, blocking the sun.

For the first time in my life, I'd made love without protection. Even with Gwen that hadn't happened. Zach had gotten started because Gwen had put the condom on wrong, not because I'd forgotten to use one. Or been so carried away I couldn't be bothered.

I grimaced. Seely had told me it was okay, but that didn't make what I'd done right. If she was on the pill…but she hadn't exactly said that, had she?

The possibility of her growing round with my child made a funny kind of pain in my chest, the sort of ache a kid gets just before Christmas, when he wants something so much he doesn't dare wish for it out loud.

Had I skipped protection because I secretly hoped she would get pregnant?

I don't usually waste time second-guessing myself, but I didn't know myself anymore. I kept changing my mind, doing things I'd decided not to do. First I'd just wanted to see Seely again. Then I'd wanted her to work for me, but had no intention of getting involved. Then I'd decided I wanted her even though she wasn't a forever kind of woman, but I planned to wait until she wasn't an employee anymore.

Now I was lying beside her, watching her sleep…after the most mind-blowing sex of my life.

Unprotected sex.

Must be some sort of midlife crisis. I wasn't the sort of man who fell in love every couple of months, and less than two weeks ago I'd been in love with Gwen. Besides, I didn't have any urge to sit around mooning over Seely, making up stories about how things ought to go between us. Nor was I blind to her flaws—and the infuriating woman had plenty of those.

I sighed with relief. No, this wasn't love. More like lust on steroids.

Hormones aside, though, I liked her. A lot. I got up in the morning looking forward to seeing her, finding out what she'd say, what she'd do that day. She was just plain fun to be with, and she mattered to me. Which was one definition of friendship, wasn't it?

Okay, so she was a friend for whom I had a bad case of the hots. I could live with that. But no more unprotected sex.

She went from asleep to awake in a single blink and smiled up at me.

"Hi, there." I couldn't brush the hair away from her face, so I brushed a kiss on her forehead. "I thought it was the guy who was supposed to fall asleep after sex."

"I love busting up stereotypes." She ran her fingers over my lips, as if seeing my smile wasn't enough. She had to touch it, too. "You break a few of those, too, you know."

"Yeah? Which ones?"

"You seem like a real macho man with your flannel shirts and jeans, your bossy ways and construction work. I really want to see you in a tool belt one of these days," she added. "But never mind that right now. The point is, macho men are supposed to have thick necks and tiny brains. They aren't supposed to be sensitive to others' feelings. Or be better read than me."

"You think I'm macho?" And was that good or bad?

"I think you're a man. One hundred percent man, the kind I didn't believe really existed."

Okay, that was good. I kissed her, taking my time about it.

"Well." She was satisfactorily short of breath when she flattened her palm on my chest. "Your heartbeat seems elevated."

"It was calm until you smiled at me."

The woman who'd played doctor so enthusiastically a few minutes ago delighted me by blushing. She shook her head, chiding me. "You're supposed to be flattened, drained, unable to even lift your head."

"I want you in my bed. Of course," I added regretfully, "I might need a little help getting there."

One eyebrow lifted. "Good as it is for my ego to know you're at least partly flattened, maybe a second round isn't a good idea. If you're hurting too much to make it back to the den—"

"Not the den." I stroked her back, enjoying the sweep of muscle and softness. "My bed is upstairs." The hospital bed was temporary. I wanted her in the bed where I slept every night, in the room where I woke up every morning.

"Stairs are not a good idea."

"But you can help, can't you?" I stared down at her, willing her to be honest this time. "I haven't figured out exactly what you do, but you damned sure do something."

Her whole face closed down. "I don't know what you're talking about."

"Dammit, if you aren't going to answer, then don't. But don't lie to me." I shoved up into a sitting position, which pretty much forced her to sit, too, or get shoved off the couch. She sat, eyeing me warily. Which made me furious. "What do I have to do to make you trust me?"

"You don't know what you're asking for."

"So tell me. Explain it to me." I looked around for my walking stick. It was across the room. Tough. I pushed to my feet anyway and started limping. "Everyone trusts me. The bank, my neighbors, people I do business with—the whole damned *town* trusts me, dammit. Ask anyone. Charlie's the charming McClain and Duncan's the mysterious one. Me, I'm Mr. Dependable." I ran a hand over my hair. "What good is having a reputation like that if you won't trust me!"

"I think you're charming." She uncoiled from the couch and came to me, naked and magnificently unconcerned about it. "Something of a mystery, too. Just when I think I've got you figured out, you pull a 180 on me." She slid her arms around my waist. "But I've only known you a week, Ben. It takes time for trust to grow."

"You trusted me with your body. But you can't trust me with the important stuff. Is that it, Seely? You don't think of this—" I ran my hand down her side "—as important?"

"Oh." That came out on a little puff of air, as if I'd punctured something. She laid her head on my shoulder. "Damn you. There goes another toppled preconception—bam! You aren't supposed to see that much."

"Was I being macho or sensitive?" I stroked her hair.

"Difficult." She sighed. "There was a time when I didn't much like my body. I developed early—and boy, did I develop. From the time I got breasts, I was never sure if men ever saw my face. Boys certainly didn't."

"Teenage boys are scum." Her hair looked so wild, and felt so soft. "They think with their second head."

"True. Well, at some point I decided that if I couldn't beat 'em, I'd join 'em." She lifted her head and looked at me, one eyebrow cocked. "I worked as a stripper when I was twenty."

The eyebrow, the expression, were all defiance. The eyes, though—they made me ache. So wild. And so soft. I kept petting. I didn't know what else to do. "So, were you any good?"

Her laugh broke in the middle. "I was damned good."

"Well, then." I slid my good arm around her waist and hugged her close.

She didn't say anything for a minute, but I felt the tension draining out of her. Then she sighed. "I was also young and stupid. Twenty is almost as arrogant as eighteen, isn't it?"

"Mmm." It felt good, holding her this way. "When I was twenty I ran off to get married."

She straightened, staring. "You're kidding. What happened?"

"We got halfway to Vegas and turned around. She started crying and wouldn't stop. Ruined the romance of it," I said dryly.

"I can't believe I didn't hear about that when everyone was filling me in on you."

"No one around here knows about it."

"Not even your family?" She grinned. "I sense real black-mail potential here."

"Seely…" I made a warning out of her name.

The amusement in her eyes softened. "She was the one you mentioned earlier, wasn't she? Did the aborted elopement end things between you?"

"No, we were still planning to get married after college." I shook my head, remembering. I'd been crazy about Bev, thought the sun rose and set on her. "We broke up when my parents died and I had to return to Highpoint. She, uh, didn't want to live here."

"Oh, Ben."

The ache in her voice made me uncomfortable. "It was a long time ago."

"She hurt you."

"She hurt, too. But she still had two years to go when it happened. Journalism degree. Not much opportunity to carve out a career as a reporter in Highpoint."

"And did she carve out a career?"

"I've seen her name in one of those weekly news maga-zines, so yeah, I guess she did. Don't look so sad. I haven't exactly been nursing a broken heart for the past twenty years. Now." I shifted my hold on her and nudged her toward the hall. "You going to help me upstairs, or do I have to crawl up there on my own?"

"Never lose track of a goal, do you?"

"Never."

That slow smile started in her eyes. "I could make you for-get about going upstairs."

"Sure of yourself, are you?" We were moving slowly, with me leaning on her enough so she'd think she was helping. Good tactics, since it caused her bare body to rub up against mine.

"Damned right I am." We'd almost reached the stairs when she slipped in front of me, making me stop. Then she just stood there smiling at me...with the tips of her breasts brushing my chest with every inhalation. "What do you think?"

"You have a point. Or two." I ran my thumb over one.

Her breath sucked in. Then she got serious about making her point.

Several long, lovely moments later a thought intruded. I nuzzled her ear. "Something I almost forgot."

"Mmm." She nuzzled my throat. "What's that?"

"You're fired."

She jerked—then shook her head, grinning. "Only you would order me to trust you, then try to fire me."

What was she grinning about? "I'll help you find another position."

"No, you won't. First, I don't need help. Second, I'm not fired."

"Uh...I don't think this one is up to you."

"Sure it is." She patted me on the arm. "You can't fire people when you're naked."

I was blinking, trying to think of a logical answer to that wholly illogical statement, when the front door swung open. And there stood my little sister. Her husband, Jack. Behind them were Gwen, Duncan and Zach. And my brother Charlie, whose voice, very dry, broke the stunned silence.

"Surprise."

The woman beside me sat down on the stairs and laughed like a loon.

Ten

"If only I'd had a camera," Annie mourned.

"And here I thought I didn't have anything to be grateful for." I took another sip of coffee. Mornings after, I reflected, can be hell. Especially if you end up spending them with your sister and brothers instead of your lover. Whom I hadn't seen alone for more than thirty seconds since I slammed the door in my family's faces yesterday.

"It's not like any of us will ever forget that moment." Charlie leaned back in his chair, his hands clasped over his skinny belly. "It was a real peak life experience."

I grunted and drank my coffee. There was no point in trying to shut them up. I'd just have to let them get it out of their systems. They hadn't been able to do that yesterday because, as much of a pain as they could be, none of them had wanted to embarrass Seely.

Me, of course, they felt free to embarrass. Obliged to, even.

Seely had been great. I smiled, remembering. Not every woman could treat meeting her lover's family for the first time while stark naked as an icebreaker. She'd pulled it off, though.

And later, she'd slipped upstairs when I wasn't watching, going to bed in her usual room without giving me a chance to change her mind about that. Without a good-night kiss, either, or a single word spoken in private. My smile faded.

She was at the grocery store now with Gwen and Zach. I planned to have a talk with her when they returned.

Annie had drawn the short straw after breakfast. So far she'd managed to avoid tripping over Doofus while she cleaned up and loaded the dishwasher. You might say that the pup was excited about all the company…just like you might say that tornadoes are windy. Jack was at the coffeepot getting a refill. He was a compact man about Duncan's height, with short brown hair and an easy grin I'd seen too much of this morning.

He'd copped my new mug, the one Annie gave me last night that read: "Men. We're just better." He leaned against the counter, took a sip from my mug, and said thoughtfully, "You know how it is when you get something you've always wanted, but didn't know you wanted? It's not as if I ever dreamed of catching Ben with his pants down."

"Who would?" Duncan asked rhetorically.

Charlie nodded. "I know what you mean. I was pretty sure he put them on one leg at a time. Not positive, but pretty sure. But as for taking them off in the middle of the day—"

"Running around the house that way," Jack said.

"Bare-ass nekkid," Charlie finished with relish.

I sighed. Charlie and Jack had been best friends back in high school. They'd driven me crazy then, too.

Annie shook her head. "The things Ben's gotten up to since we left. Shocking. I had no idea."

"You've gotten up to a few things yourself." Charlie waggled his eyebrows. "Or so the presence of little Matilda indicates."

Annie got that soft look on her face I'd seen last night, the one that made her look so different from the freckle-faced tomboy I'd watched grow up. Her hand went to her stomach. If I looked closely, I could see the slight bulge beneath her T-shirt. "We may not have picked out names yet, but trust me—Matilda is *not* an option."

Annie and Jack had made their big announcement at the surprise party last night—a combination get-well-soon and belated-birthday bash. For me. That's why they'd all shown up like they had.

The surprise part had worked out a little too well, but the party itself had been great. The best part, of course, had been learning I'd have a niece or nephew in just over six months. She and Jack would be staying Stateside for quite some time, and…I swallowed the lump that kept coming back.

Annie was going to have a baby. My little sister. Imagine that.

Was there was any chance I'd be seeing Seely's tummy get round that way? She'd said not, but…

"Gertrude," Duncan suggested, straight-faced. "That's a good, solid name."

Charlie nodded. "Or Alphonse, if it's a boy. A boy named Alphonse would be sensitive, and I know that's important to you."

"Jack," Annie said, "kill those two pea-brains for me, will you?"

"Pour me some more coffee first," I said, pushing my empty mug toward him. "Before anything gets broken."

"Like me," Jack said, bringing the carafe to the table. "I can take Charlie—"

"Ha!" Charlie said.

"But Duncan?" Jack shook his head as he refilled my cup. "You know I'd do anything for you, love, but this isn't a good time for me to go into the hospital."

I started to reach for the cup he held out. The sling kept the movement to a tiny jerk. Dammit—I'd forgotten. I took the mug in my left hand and sipped.

"Something wrong with the coffee, Ben?"

"No, it's good." Not as good as Seely's, but that wasn't what had brought a scowl to my face.

I could have used my right hand. If the sling hadn't reminded me, I would have. This morning I'd woken up reaching for a woman I'd never slept beside, which was weird enough…but I'd been reaching with my right arm.

My shoulder had barely twinged. And my knee didn't hurt at all.

I'd experimented. I couldn't lift my arm over my head yet, but I could raise it up to my shoulder. It was weak, but I could use it for little things like getting dressed. Brushing my teeth. Getting my sock back from Doofus.

No way should I have been able to do all that. After pulling on my jeans I'd sat on the hospital bed, feeling cold and sick. I don't know why it shook me up so badly. I'd been pretty sure Seely had done something impossible on the mountain…but there's knowing and there's *knowing*. I guess part of me just flat hadn't believed it. Hadn't wanted to believe it.

The world wasn't the same place it used to be. Reality wasn't what I'd always believed it was. Maybe Seely's granny really was a witch. Maybe she'd turn me into a toadstool if I messed with her granddaughter.

"Hey." A hand passed in front of my face. "You in there?"

I swatted at Annie's hand but missed.

She pulled up the chair beside me and sat. Duncan had left

the room; Jack and Charlie were arguing about something. "So how are you, really?" Annie asked.

"Fine." Better than should have been possible, but I wasn't going to go into that. Seely didn't want anyone to know—hell, she wouldn't even talk to me about it. Considering how long I'd sat on that bed with my hands shaking, I could see why she wanted it kept secret. "How about you? Any morning sickness?"

"I'm healthy as a horse. Which is more than you can say right now, but that wasn't what I meant. I'm worried about you."

"Me?" I shook my head. "You're not making sense."

"Neither are you. That's what worries me. Ben." She put her hand on my arm. "All teasing aside, it isn't like you to get naked with an employee. I like Seely, but—"

"Good. Fine. I'm glad you like her. Leave it at that."

"But something she said last night made it obvious she isn't planning to stay in Highpoint. And she isn't…" She sighed. "I don't know how to put this."

"Don't put it at all." I was getting annoyed. "Look, do I tell you how to handle your relationship with Jack?"

She stared. "You have amnesia? The knock on your head loosened your brains?"

"Okay, okay. Maybe I did make a few comments back when you two first got serious."

"You threatened to break parts of his body."

"He was kissing you! Had his hands all over the place."

"We were married."

"Yeah, well, I didn't know that at the time. After that—"

"You butted in every chance you got for a good long while. And as mad as that made me, I knew you did it because you cared. So I'm claiming the same privilege. Because I care, too."

Damn. She had me pinned.

"But I'm going to try for a little more tact than you used." Her grin flashed briefly. "I guess what I really want to know is whether this is a fling, a just-for-fun affair. Because it doesn't look like one."

"What is this, feminine intuition? You haven't even been home a full day yet."

She snorted. "Feminine intuition is the amazing ability women have to see what's under our noses. From the moment I saw you two together—oh. Not the very *first* moment. Memorable as that was." Again the grin, but again it faded. Annie shook her head. "It's the way you look at her, the way…you're just different with her, Ben. That's what worries me. Because—"

Doofus leaped up, yapping loudly, and ran toward the front of the house. "They must be back," I said, relieved, and shoved my chair back. "I'll give them a hand with the groceries."

Annie's hand closed around my wrist. "You'll sit. You're supposed to be convalescing, remember? Though I must say, you're doing better than I'd expected."

Better than I'd expected, too.

"Which leads back to what I've been trying to say. I hope you're not in too deep, because I don't think Seely plans to stay around. She told me last night you wouldn't need her much longer."

Not need her? Was the woman crazy?

I shoved to my feet. We definitely needed to talk.

It was afternoon before I was able to cut Seely out of the herd. Me, Gwen and Annie were sitting out on the deck. The weather was crisp and clear—jacket weather, if you weren't running around with five-year-old boys. Which Duncan, Charlie and Jack were doing, in a scaled-down version of softball. The twins had been invited over to wear Zach out. So far it wasn't working.

Gwen and Annie were talking about sex. They'd started out discussing pregnancy, but somehow that segued into sex. I was pretending I wasn't listening.

Not that it isn't an interesting subject, but dammit, Annie was my little sister. Besides, a man who gets into a discussion of that subject with more than one woman at a time is asking for trouble. They'll embarrass the hell out of you. When women bunch up in packs, they have no shame.

Seely had been talking with them, too, until a moment ago. She'd gone into the house to use the bathroom.

I stood. I'd given her a thirty-second head start. That was enough. "Think I'll grab another beer. Anyone else want one?"

Gwen rose to her feet. "I'll get it."

"No, you won't." I headed for the kitchen door.

"I'll take one," Charlie called from the scrap of cardboard that was serving as pitcher's mound. "Soon as I strike Jack out, these guys are dust." Jack and his two smaller teammates hooted their opinions of this prediction. I nodded and went inside.

I was leaning against the door to the laundry room when the bathroom door opened. Seely's hand flew to her chest. "Ben!"

Her hair was down, and oh, Lord, but I liked it that way. Her sweater was green with little buttons down the front. I liked those buttons, too. Though it didn't look like I was going to get a chance to mess with either her hair or her buttons anytime soon. "Surprised? You shouldn't be. You must have known you couldn't avoid me forever."

Her eyebrows expressed polite disbelief. "You may have noticed there are a few more people staying here now? I've been busy."

"We need to talk."

"Okay. You can talk to me while I peel apples." She started for the kitchen.

Dammit, she was doing it again—holding me at a distance. Avoiding me even when I was standing right in front of her. Maybe making love hadn't meant anything to her. Maybe she regretted it. Maybe she did plan to leave soon.

And maybe talk wasn't what I needed. I took two quick strides and slapped my hand on the wall beside her, stopping her.

She frowned at me. "I need to get the pies started."

I leaned in and kissed her.

She didn't push me away. Her lips were warm and soft...and they quivered beneath mine in a single, telling spasm of uncertainty. Seely, always so sure of herself, so dauntlessly confident, was frightened.

Suddenly I could admit I'd been scared, too. All day. Like thunder in the distance, fear had rumbled away deep inside, never drawing so close I was forced to notice it. Never going away, either.

I touched her bottom lip with my tongue, telling her it was okay, that I was scared, too. I feathered kisses across her cheek so she'd know I meant to be careful with her—not just her body, but all those achy inside places. Her breath caught. I brushed my lips across hers one more time, leaned my forehead on hers and sighed. "I've been wanting to do that all day."

"I don't think Annie and your brothers would have fainted if you'd kissed me in front of them."

"No, but they would have been hugely amused if you'd belted me for it. And I wasn't sure you wouldn't."

"Did you really think that? I didn't mean..." She shook her head, dismissing whatever she'd been about to say, and put a hand on my chest. "I'm sorry. I guess I've been running scared."

"Good. I'd hate to be the only one."

Her smile flickered. "I like your family."

"Me, too. Most of the time. What's wrong?"

"Foolishness. And I guess I'm a little jealous. You know I told you I was an only child? Well, my mother was, too. That's my whole family—me, Daisy and Granny."

I studied her face. She was telling the truth…but maybe not all of the truth. I touched her cheek gently. "Did you ever wonder if you had more family somewhere? Not the grandmother from hell, but your father might have married, had more kids."

Her eyelids lowered, shielding her eyes. "He did."

That sent a jolt to my stomach. "Well, hell. Did you know that when you came to Highpoint?"

Seely nodded. "He sent Daisy a birth announcement. Can you imagine that? No letter, just the printed announcement."

"Okay, he may be worse than a noodle." I hesitated. "You have a brother or sister?"

"Brother. Half brother, I mean." She sighed and laid her head on my shoulder. "I toyed with the idea of introducing myself, but when I stayed with the judge and Granny Dearest all those years ago, my father never brought his new wife and son with him when he came up on weekends. So my brother may not know I exist."

"You came all the way to Highpoint, but didn't do anything about meeting him?"

"Oh, I did something. Being a bright, mature woman, I stalked him."

I didn't mean to laugh. It snuck out.

"I agree. Pretty ridiculous. I checked out where he works, where he lives. I'd just about talked myself into going up to his door, but kept driving around his house.

Then someone else pulled up. I saw them together. All of them—my father, his wife, their son. They were…complete. A unit. I decided I had to either fish or cut bait." She shrugged. "I cut bait. That's when your brother found me at the bus station."

"Thank God he did."

She nodded against my shoulder. "It hurt. Seeing them together hurt. I didn't expect that."

"Yeah. I guess it would." I smoothed her hair back from her face.

"I came here because I was curious, not because I had any stupid ideas of a family reunion. I wouldn't have been hurt if I'd remembered that."

"There you go, being human." I shook my head and snuggled her more firmly against me. "Got to watch that. Leads to all sorts of complications."

She snorted and slid both arms around my waist. For a minute we just stood there, holding on to each other. It probably looked as if I was comforting her, but the comfort went both ways.

Fear wasn't a rumble on the horizon anymore—it was right up in my face. Seely had no intention of staying in Highpoint. Under the circumstances, I couldn't blame her. But I couldn't lose her. All at once that was blindingly obvious. Somehow I had to make her want to stay.

The thing to do, then, was to change the circumstances. But first things first. "I'm moving back into my bedroom tonight."

She pulled back to study my face, her eyebrows raised. "You've decided your sister and brother-in-law should share a twin bed?"

With all the company, the only bedroom left was the one that used to be Annie's. It was Zach's room now. Annie and Jack were in my bedroom, Charlie was in his—at least, it had been his until he quit trucking a few months ago to find himself and ended up in Arizona. And Seely was in Duncan's old room.

My heart started pounding. Oh, yeah, I was scared. Foolishly, over-the-top scared. "There's a double bed in your room. If you move in with me, they can have that one."

She didn't exactly fall on my neck with enthusiasm for the idea. "Define 'move in.'"

"Sleep in my bed. Take over the closet. Argue over who gets custody of the remote." I ran my hand along the length of her hair where it spilled over her shoulder, and my voice dropped. "Be there when I wake up and reach out for you."

Her eyes were troubled. "Ben…"

"I reached for you this morning and you weren't there."

She swallowed. "I thought you didn't believe in living together."

"I changed my mind." *Please,* I thought—maybe at God, maybe at Seely. *Please.*

That slow smile started in her eyes, spreading over the rest of her face like sunlight easing up over the rim of the world. "Changing your mind…is that anything like admitting you were wrong?"

"Pretty close."

"In that case…" She slid her arms around my neck. "I suppose a man who can admit he was wrong deserves some kind of reward."

"Is that a yes?"

"It is."

Several minutes later she was pressed against the wall, one leg curled around my thigh. Various things were unfastened. We were both breathing hard.

"Oh, boy," she said, resting her forehead against my shoulder and letting her leg slide back down. "We are not going to do this here."

"Right." I'd forgotten where we were, forgotten about my brothers, my sister and sister-in-law, my son and his friends…I was going to be really worried about my loss of control. Later. Maybe tomorrow. Right now I didn't have enough blood left in my head to scrape together a thought that didn't involve the wall, the fullness of the breast I cupped and whether it was possible to do what I wanted with only one arm.

I dragged more air in, let it out. "About that pie…apple, you said?"

Her laugh was shaky. "You are *such* a man. Here, help me put back together some of the bits you unfastened."

"I may as well peel apples. I can't go back outside yet, not in this condition. My brothers would never let me hear the end of it." They'd probably rag me anyway, but if I went out there now I'd hear way too many cracks about hauling lumber around in my jeans.

We got her bra and sweater fastened, and her jeans—which I didn't remember undoing—and my jeans, which I *know* I hadn't unsnapped—and headed for the kitchen hand in hand. I was limping a little for the first time that day.

Which reminded me. "You haven't given me any trouble about my knee and the stairs. I guess you knew it's pretty much healed."

She slid me a long, level glance. And didn't say a word.

"I'd complain about how long it took you," Charlie said, taking the bottle I held out, "but Seely has more to bitch about. You were in there too long for retrieving a couple beers, not long enough for anything else. Not if you did things right."

"You want to drink that beer or wear it?"

He grinned, lazy and obnoxious. "You're big, but I'm faster. Especially with half your body parts not working right. Speaking of which…" He waggled his eyebrows.

"Works fine," I said mildly, and took a swig of my own beer.

"Glad to hear it." Charlie tilted his bottle up.

The softball game had broken up while I was in the kitchen with Seely. Gwen and Annie were inside helping get the last few things done; the women had agreed to handle the preparation if the men took care of the ribs and the cleanup. Duncan was on his way home to shower and change into his uniform. He'd be back to eat his share before he started his shift.

I needed to talk to him, but it could wait. Right now I felt too good to worry about anything. The sky was that drenched shade of blue that makes me feel crisp and happy, as if all that color were pouring down into me, opening me up. The ribs smelled incredible. Zach and the twins were building a fort with the help of their uncle Jack, the construction engineer. And Seely would sleep in my bed tonight.

Charlie and I stood under the big oak next to the swing I'd hung for Zach, drinking beer and watching the kids. It's a good yard for kids—big, with plenty of thick grass, but a few bare spots, too. Kids need dirt. They need places that aren't all fixed up so they can build and tear down, dream and dig and make a mess.

Dreams…I'd thought I had given up on them, but they're hard to kill. This yard, like the house, was big enough to welcome a lot of kids. I was picturing a curly-haired little girl in the tire swing when Charlie said, "I like your lady."

My lady. That sounded good. "She's something, isn't she?" I remembered what Seely had said about men not noticing her face. "And I'm not talking about—"

"I didn't get a good look at them," Charlie assured me

"You closed the door too fast. Anyway, that wasn't what I meant. Though I do have to say that if Seely stays around long, you may die young, but you'll die happy."

"Yeah." Making sure she stayed around was the trick. "I'm going to marry her."

He spewed beer all over. After he finished choking, he gave me a wary look. "You, ah, mentioned that to her?"

"Not yet." First I had to deal with the situation that had made her want to leave Highpoint.

I had a plan for that.

Eleven

At ten-thirty that night I was pacing my bedroom, which wasn't smart. I ought to stretch out in the big, comfortable bed I'd been missing and save my energy for more important things. But I couldn't settle.

The shower in the bathroom off my bedroom was running. Seely was in it.

I paused by the bed and scowled at the door to the bathroom. I was as nervous as a new English recruit watching the French form up outside a tiny village in Belgium known as Waterloo.

I grimaced. Make that as nervous as a bridegroom.

I'd always thought that when a woman moved her clothes into my closet, she'd be my wife. This living-together business was new territory for me. It didn't help that it was taking place under the amused, worried or just plain nosy eyes of my brothers and sister. Jaws had dropped when I'd announced the room changes over spareribs and coleslaw. By the time we got to the apple pie I'd almost lost my appetite.

Why did they all have to act so amazed? It's not as if anyone could have mistaken me for a virgin. I'd dated. I'd had affairs, too, some of them lasting awhile. Shoot, I'd had a fiancée back in college. Okay, so maybe my family didn't know Bev and I had been engaged. They'd known we were seeing each other. You'd think they'd have guessed there was sex involved.

What I'd never had, I realized, was a *relationship*.

No wonder I was nervous.

Relationship is a woman's word. It means that you're serious about each other, but not serious enough to get married. It means "maybe," not yes. It means that when there are problems, you're supposed to talk, work things out. In other words, make up the rules as you go along.

Jesus. I ran a hand over my hair. She sure was taking a long time in the shower.

I knew very well it was one thing to decide to marry Seely, another to pull it off. Especially when she thought she was cursed to love unhappily. She claimed she didn't believe in the curse, but I was pretty sure that deep down she did.

But maybe that wasn't such a bad deal. Women mostly liked me, some of them enough to go to bed with me. But they didn't fall head-over-heels in love, and I didn't have a clue how to make that happen. I had other things going for me, though. I was dependable. Dependable isn't sexy, but it helps when you're in for the long haul. Besides, Seely and I had the passion thing down. I wasn't going to worry about that aspect.

I could offer her a home, but I wasn't sure she wanted one. Does security matter to a woman who's been drifting around the country? But fidelity—surely that meant something. I was aces at fidelity.

And she liked me. Aside from our fireworks in bed, she liked being with me. So I had plenty to build on, I assured myself.

The sound of the water shut off. My head swivelled toward the bathroom door, but she would have more woman-stuff to do, I reminded myself. Hair, lotion, things like that. I resumed my pacing.

My gaze fell on the pile I'd brought up from downstairs—the junk that had been sitting next to my hospital bed. Including the books I'd ordered, which I'd gotten out of sight fast when my family descended on us. Books like *The Laying On of Hands*—there were two with that title—*Hands of Healing, The Women's Book of Healing* and, God help me, *Chakras, Auras and the Healing Energy of the Body.*

My fingers went to my shoulder, where a gauze pad covered the rapidly healing wound. I wasn't wearing the sling. Didn't need it anymore, though I still used it when others were around so no one asked questions I couldn't answer.

My lips tightened. I didn't mind keeping her secret, but I damned sure wanted to know what that secret was. I was pretty sure that one of the relationship rules involved being honest and open with your partner. Seely was going to have to give me some answers.

I just hoped those answers didn't involve chakras or auras.

I grimaced and caught a glimpse of my reflection in the mirror. That gave me something new to worry about. I've always been fit, and Seely seemed to like the way I was built, so I didn't think my body was a problem. But maybe I should have worn the stupid pajamas. Boxers weren't exactly romantic.

The hell with it. Normally I didn't even wear boxers to bed, much less pajamas. If a man couldn't be comfortable in his own bedroom, he—

The bathroom door opened. Seely smiled at me.

Her nightgown was made like a man's shirt, a satiny blue-green shirt that shimmered over her breasts like sunlight on water and left her legs mostly bare. Her hair frizzed around her face and spilled over her shoulders, excited by the humidity from her shower.

Her smile was shy. "Hi, sailor. Looking for a girl to show you a good time?"

I exhaled in relief. "Good. You're nervous, too."

She gave a startled laugh. "You want me to be nervous?"

"I don't want to be the only one who swallowed Mexican jumping beans." Seeing her nerves settled mine down. I moved to her and put my arms around her waist. "I like your nightgown."

"Good." Her lips tilted mischievously and she tucked her fingertips into the waistband of my shorts. "I see you're a flannel kind of a guy, all the way."

"Flannel's warm." I kissed her cheek. "And soft." I kissed the other cheek. "I like warm, soft things."

"Mmm." Her eyes were slumberous and sexy. "If I didn't know better, I'd say you were trying to distract me from my nerves."

"How am I doing?" This time I touched her lips with mine.

"Pretty good."

My body was making suggestions about the curves and softness nestled against me. I could tell she was aroused, too. But for a moment we just stood there smiling at each other.

She pulled away to wander the room, touching things as if she were getting acquainted. "It's funny. Sometimes it seems as if I've known you for ages, but I haven't. I was struck by that when I came out just now—how short a time I've known you. I've never been in your bedroom at the same time you were." She shook her head. "Even for a couple of impetuous souls like us, things have moved pretty fast, haven't they?"

"Wait a minute. I am not impetuous."

"No?" Her mouth twitched. "What do you call hiring me without checking my references? Or asking me to live with you when you've only known me ten days?"

"A good decision and a great one. I'm decisive, not impulsive."

That made her laugh. It was a good sound. "I like your room. Very masculine, but in a comfortable way. A touch old-fashioned. This lamp is a surprise, though." She touched the shade on the lamp by the bed. "It's lovely, but quite feminine."

"It was my mother's. I kind of like keeping her lamp where I can see it. She was so tickled when she bought it—it's hand-painted china."

Her ready smile tilted her lips up. "You're sentimental."

"It's not sentimental to respect the past."

"I like sentimental." She came back to me and linked her arms around my waist. "I think I'm ready to be fired now."

"Ah…" I blinked a couple times. "Because we aren't naked yet?"

"Because you don't need nursing care anymore. I can't justify drawing a salary for scrubbing your back and nagging you to take care of yourself."

Those were things a wife did. I gripped her waist. "I'll scrub your back, too."

"It's a deal."

I kissed her like I meant it this time. When I lifted my head, it wasn't because I wanted to. I've always preferred action to words, and my body was definitely not in the mood for verbal communication.

But I couldn't let this go. "One more thing we need to talk about. Why *don't* I need nursing care?"

She went still—and her face, dammit, closed down.

"I don't need the sling anymore. I ought to, but I don't. My knee is almost normal. I want to understand."

She pulled away and paced. "Why can't you just accept it? Stop asking questions, stop trying to make it fit your logical world, stop reading—oh, yes, I've seen that pile of books. Why can't you leave it alone?"

"Because you won't talk about it. You won't even tell me why you won't talk about it!"

"I want to feel normal! Is that so hard to understand?" Her voice turned wistful. "You do that for me, Ben. Here, with you and your family, I feel deliciously normal. Ordinary. As if I fit." She held out a hand. "Is it wrong to want to pretend for a while that I'm like everyone else?"

"You do fit." My throat closed up around the words, so I went to her and pulled her close. "You fit just fine."

She held on tight. "I could use some more distracting."

"I can do that." I lifted her hair with both hands, smoothing it away from her face. "I'm pretty damned distracted myself." Which might be the first lie I'd ever told her. I was hard, I was aching, but I wasn't distracted.

But pretense was what she wanted, wasn't it? She met my mouth gladly.

For the first time I was sure that she needed me…but what she needed from me was pretense, like the game of doctor we'd played the first time we made love. But no one wins when you play at denial. I knew that, and still I let her do it.

The most extraordinary woman I'd ever known longed to feel normal. It just about broke my heart.

"Ben. Ben!"

Someone shook my shoulder. I jerked and woke from nightmare.

"You were dreaming," Seely said. "Not a good dream, from the sound of it."

"No. It wasn't." I rolled onto my back and scrubbed my face. My skin was clammy.

The house was as silent as an old house ever gets, heavy with that dead-end-of-the-night feel. The old casement clock on the chest of drawers was ticking away. I heard the rustle of the covers as Seely propped herself up. I couldn't see her, except as a paler smudge against the darkness. But her hand was warm on my chest, and her hair tickled my shoulder.

"You want to tell me about it?" she asked. "Or would that violate the Tough Guy Code?"

"Not much to tell."

"Well, which sort of nightmare was it? The kind where you're being chased by hairy critters with big teeth? Or maybe a version of my personal favorite—the one where I show up for algebra class in time for the big test, but somehow neglected to get dressed first."

Okay, she'd made me smile. I reached up and tugged on one long strand of hair. "No great hairy monsters. This was more reality based."

"And…?"

I shrugged. "I was crawling along the mountain again, only I'd lost track of which way was up, so I wasn't getting anywhere."

"Reality-based nightmares are the pits." She rubbed my chest in small circles. "What happened to you was the pits, too."

"Yeah." In the nightmare I'd kept moving, just like in reality. But I hadn't been able to tell uphill from down, so moving hadn't helped. And in the nightmare, Seely hadn't found me. I'd been dying—lost, cold, alone and dying. "I guess I have to expect a few bad dreams after such a close call."

"Maybe so." Her fingers began playing with my chest hair. "Um…you need some help getting back to sleep? I'm wide awake now, too."

I felt raw, unsteady. Words seemed too frail and distant to navigate by, so I cupped her nape with my hand and brought her head down for a kiss. At the touch of her lips, need shuddered through me.

She was here. That's all I could think—Seely was real. She was in my arms, in my bed. The nightmare was false, because Seely was here.

Sex arranges itself in all sorts of ways, a grand variety of positions, styles and speeds. I wasn't thinking about style or variety then. I wasn't thinking at all. It was instinct that had me rolling her onto her back, a primitive need to cover her body with my own. It was hunger that compelled me, but a hunger unlike any I'd known.

Seely was under me. Her hands welcomed me as our legs and tongues tangled. My heart drummed an exultant riff and I took my mouth lower, drifting kisses along the cord of her neck.

She feathered her fingertips over my shoulder, where a gauze pad protected the wound. Her voice was soft and none too steady. "I should have known you'd want to be on top sooner rather than later, but your shoulder—"

"I'll be careful." I licked my way down the slope of her breast. She shivered. "Your knee…"

"Doesn't hurt a bit." Which wasn't possible, but I wasn't going to question her now.

There was no moon that night, and my room is at the back of the house. The darkness was rich and complete, a prickling along my skin, a weightless cover woven of possibilities. In that darkness, driven by a need that both was and wasn't physical, I lost track of surfaces.

Here reality was dimensional, bodies meeting and moving in space. And as with my crawl up the mountain, reality broke up into parts—but this time each part seemed to hold the whole. I found Seely in the curve of her thigh, and the tender skin inside her elbow. She was the air that moved through my lungs, the soft cry I heard as I sucked at her breast, the hand sifting my hair. She was the dip of her navel, and the musk filling the air as I parted her inner lips and kissed her there.

At last the urgency became irresistible, pooling in one place like my blood. I braced myself over her and pushed inside. She was hot and wet, and her inner walls began contracting around me before I was fully in.

She called my name. She held on to me as my body thrust and thrust again. My own explosion hit, the universe cracking over me like a woman cracks an egg on the side of a bowl, a white-hot blow that split me open and spilled me out.

A few minutes later I fell asleep holding her and being held, neither of us having spoken another word. If I dreamed again, I didn't know it.

Twelve

One week later Annie and Jack were in Denver looking for a larger apartment; Charlie was in Arizona, planning landscapes and planting them; Zach was at Mrs. Bradshaw's; and Seely was checking out a job in the office of the elementary school near the house.

Me, I was back at work. Only for a few hours, true, but it felt great to be sitting at my desk in a chair that knew the ins and outs of my body as intimately as any spouse. My sling was draped over the back of that chair. I'd taken it off as soon as Manny left for the Patterson site, and would put it back on before I left the office. But I didn't need it. Not anymore.

In the past two hours I'd signed a few checks, talked to two suppliers and looked over bids from subcontractors. But right now I was staring out the window, wishing I was with Manny.

Deceiving Seely made my stomach hurt.

Not that I'd lied to her, but there's more to honesty than avoiding a spoken lie. I was about to do something behind her back.

I sighed, punched in the number I'd gotten from directory assistance, then listened to the phone ringing on the other end. It rang seven times.

At last a cheerful female voice sang, "Hello! This is Daisy, live and in person. Do you hate those blasted machines as much as I do?"

"Ah—I'm not too fond of them."

"Especially the ones that make you keep punching in numbers. 'Punch three if you'd like to place an order. Punch four if you hate broccoli. Punch five if you've ever been arrested.'"

I found myself smiling. "Punch five and you'll probably wind up arrested and hospitalized. Someone's sure to punch back."

She laughed. "Good point. So who is this?"

"My name is Ben McClain. I called because—"

"Seely's man! How wonderful of you to call. She has a rule, you know. I'm not allowed to interrogate anyone she dates for at least a month. But you called me, so that makes it all right, don't you think?"

"You want to interrogate me?"

"I prefer to think of it as a little get-acquainted chat."

If Seely's mother wanted to know about my intentions or my bank account, I should be okay. I had the idea Daisy Jones didn't operate on the usual channels, however. "If you want to know my astrological sign, I haven't the foggiest idea."

"Oh, I don't cast horoscopes anymore. What's your favorite member of the vegetable kingdom?"

Vegetable kingdom? I shook my head and told myself to play along. "There's this oak tree in the backyard…I guess you could call it my favorite."

"You picked a tree." She sounded delighted. "The name of your first pet?"

"Rocky. Do you really do this to anyone Seely dates?"

"Most people get used to it," she assured me. "Tell me about Rocky. Was he a dog or a turtle?"

"Why those two options?" I asked, disconcerted.

"Hedging my bets. Rocky sounds like a turtle, but I tend to think of boys and dogs."

I told her about Rocky—a box turtle I'd found when I was three. Then I told her my favorite time of day; the one food I wouldn't eat if someone tied me down and stuck pins in me; which former president I'd like to meet, and why; and what kind of vehicle I drove.

She liked trucks. Knew quite a bit about them, too, which didn't sound like any New-Age witch I'd ever imagined. But then, I wasn't clear on whether she considered herself a witch.

While we talked trucks I looked out the window at the new Dodge Ram sitting in my parking spot. The insurance company had paid up in record time, and yesterday Seely had gone with me to select the new pickup. I'd intended to get a white one, like usual, but had to admit the dark blue looked good.

A truck wasn't a good family vehicle, though. Maybe I should trade the old Chevy in on something newer....

"We may have to agree to disagree about Fords," Seely's mom said. "Now, to get back to my questions—how old were you when you had your first sexual experience?"

I didn't quite swallow my tongue. "You've got to be kidding."

Daisy's chuckle was low and wicked and made me think of her daughter. "You'd be surprised how often people answer that one. I suppose I should stop tormenting you and let you get it out of your system. Whatever you called to ask me, that is."

"Why do you think I called to ask you something?"

"Why else would you call? Unless Seely was ill or injured, and she isn't."

I didn't ask why she was sure of that. What if she told me, and I believed her? "Seely has a brother. I need to know how to get in touch with him."

There was a long pause. "Seely knows his name. Why don't you ask her?"

I ran a hand over my hair. "I'll level with you. I want to talk to the man, and I don't want Seely to know about it. Not right away, at least. It would be wrong to get his name from her if I'm going to do something sneaky with the information."

"An interesting ethical distinction. Why do you want to talk to him?"

"She's got issues." I pushed to my feet, unable to be still. "She doesn't think the deal with her father is supposed to bother her anymore, but it does. She was going to leave Highpoint without talking to him or her brother. That's not right."

"And you know what's right for her?"

"Not about her father," I admitted. "She's got some heavy-duty feelings there, and with reason. I don't understand how a man can ignore his own child. I can't sort that out for her. But her brother…she won't have the same kind of old hurt tied up around meeting him."

"Mmm. I see what you mean—the expectations would be different. But, Ben, meddling is seldom wise."

"Seely said she came to Highpoint because she was curious. I think it's more than that. Whatever pulled her here, I don't think she's fixed it yet. I think she needs to meet her brother. Find out if he smiles slowly, the way she does. If they watch the same shows or eat the same foods. If she likes him."

"He's a half-brother. She may not see that much of herself in him."

I shrugged impatiently. "Half, whole, he's still family. Does he know about her?"

"I don't know." Another pause. "I've believed for some time that she needs to resolve some of those issues you mentioned. I hadn't thought about going in the back door, so to speak, via her brother. It might work."

Relief broke over me in a grin. "You're going to help."

"I never claimed to be wise. His name is Jonathan. Jonathan Burns."

"Thanks." Still grinning, I reached for the phone book and started thumbing through it. There was more I wanted to ask, but I wasn't sure how to bring it up. "Ah...Seely told me about her grandmother."

"Mrs. Burns?"

"No, I met that one. It wasn't fun." There it was: Jonathan S. Burns, 1117 W. Thornbird. I closed the phone book. "What I mean is, Seely told me about your mother being a—" I swallowed "—a witch."

"Did she, now?"

"If she wasn't supposed to say anything—"

"No, I was just surprised. She doesn't talk about our family's heritage to many people."

"Yeah, well, speaking of the family heritage...hell. She just pulled up. I'd better go."

"Don't worry about it," she said soothingly. "I was just going to tell you to discuss it with Seely."

I was irked. "You might try letting me ask a question before you answer."

"It's more fun this way. I noticed that you had a hard time saying the word witch."

"It's a weird word. Listen, Ms. Jones—"

"Daisy."

"Daisy, then. I really have to go."

"Seely's been hurt in the past by people who couldn't accept her."

I'd suspected as much. "She wants to feel normal. I don't know what—ah, nice talking to you," I said hastily as the door opened.

Seely cocked an eyebrow at me as she strolled into my office. She had a satisfied look that made me hope the interview had gone well.

"I'll call you later," I told her mother firmly.

Daisy chuckled. "I'm tempted to ask you to put Seely on, but I'll resist. Bye, Ben. Call anytime."

I disconnected, put the phone down and gave Seely what I hoped was an encouraging smile. "Either you got the job, or you're really glad to see me."

She laughed, came up and put her arms around my neck. "Both."

"Good to know our schools aren't being run by idiots." I gave her the kiss her uptilted face invited. "We'll celebrate. Want to go to the resort for supper and sneer at Vic?"

"I like the way your mind works. But no business talk. You're not supposed to be working at all until you've been to the doctor for your checkup. Which is Tuesday, right?"

The pleasure drained out of me. "I canceled it. I'm not going to the doctor, Seely."

"You..." Her voice trailed off and her gaze flickered to the sling hanging on my chair. She swallowed and looked away. "I never meant to force you into some kind of coverup."

She was feeling guilty. Hell. And for the wrong reason—she *ought* to feel bad about not telling me everything, not because I was helping her keep her secret. "It's no big deal. I don't need to see the doctor to know I'm healing just fine."

Her head gave a single shake. "You shouldn't be forced to lie for me."

"I doubt I'll have to. Anyone who finds out I didn't go in for my checkup will put it down to me being ornery and lecture me. Hey." I put my fingers beneath her chin and tilted her face toward me. "This is not a big deal. It's not like I'm some kind of saint who never told a lie."

Her expression was odd, sort of sad and tender and wry all at once. "Not a saint, no. More like George Washington. You can't tell a lie without it troubling that great, big integrity bone that runs alongside your spine. Which is why I wondered…" Her eyes searched mine. "If I didn't know better, I'd say you were looking guilty when I came in. Maybe about whoever was on the phone?"

It took me a beat too long to reply. "Good thing you know better, isn't it? Come on." I reached out and snagged my sling. "Let's get me rigged up so we can go home and primp for our night out."

She laughed, as I'd hoped, and offered to loan me some lipstick. I shook my head and said I couldn't use her colors because I was a winter—a bit of female jargon I'd overheard. That really tickled her.

And all the while I was thinking about secrets, hers and mine, and that secrets were bad for a relationship, worse for a marriage. Mine wouldn't be a secret for long, though. Once I figured out a way to get Seely and her brother together, I wouldn't have anything to hide. But hers…

I gave her another kiss and headed for my new, dark-blue truck. She climbed into her car and we drove home sort of together, sort of alone, each in our own vehicle. Which pretty much summed up this whole relationship business, I thought gloomily.

* * *

"Look, Daddy! Look at me!"

Zach had promoted me from Dad to Daddy a couple of months ago. Whenever he called me that, my chest got warm and tight. "I'm watching," I told him from my spot on the other side of the cedar fence. "You're way up there, all right."

He and the twins were all over Mrs. Bradshaw's jungle gym, bundled up against the chill. I'd meant to bring him home until it was time for Gwen to come for him, but the three kids were having too much fun.

"So where's your pretty lady?" Mrs. B. asked.

"Inside, gilding the lily."

"Looks like you did some gilding, too. You're looking mighty dressed up."

"Now and then I leave off the flannel." My sports coat was suede the color of old buckskin, and tailored western-style. It had been a gift from Annie last Christmas. She called it "very Robert Redford." I don't know about that, since I doubt there are many men on the face of the planet who look less like Robert Redford than I do. But I was secretly proud of the way it looked. And I could wear it with jeans, which made it just about perfect. "We're going to the resort for dinner."

"Good for you. About time you took her someplace nice." Faded blue eyes twinkled behind the lavender-framed glasses. "You thinking of keeping this one, Ben? I like her."

"I'd tell you to mind your own business," I said amiably, "but I hate to waste my breath."

She chuckled. Naomi Bradshaw was a little dab of a woman with leathery skin and the most noticing eyes of anyone I knew. I guess thirty years of keeping track of kids will do that for you. She'd raised her own after her husband walked out, plus having had a hand in raising any number of other people's kids.

She was also the nosiest woman I knew. "Good to see that you're not mooning over Gwen anymore."

I scowled. "You've got a helluva imagination. And no tact."

"Don't have to be tactful with someone whose diapers I changed."

"Try another one. I was seven when you moved in next door, and you didn't start keeping children for another couple of years after that."

"The principle's the same. You haven't changed much since then—still stubborn as a mule." She shook her head. "Guess you thought the sling would mess up the lines of your pretty jacket."

Damn. I'd forgotten all about the stupid thing when I changed clothes. I didn't want her wondering why I was doing so well. "I don't need the damned sling," I growled.

"Stubborn as any mule," she repeated. "Better put it on so you don't start out your evening with an argument, because unless I miss my guess, Seely isn't…"

"Mrs. B.?" I straightened. She had an odd look on her face, as if she'd turned queasy. "You okay?"

"Fine." She waved one hand vaguely, but she didn't look any better. And she sounded winded. "Just a little…" She shook her head, looking confused. "I feel funny."

Alarmed, I said, "You go inside and lie down. I'll round up the boys and bring them over here."

"Don't be silly. Their moms will be here in twenty minutes or so. That's soon enough to coddle myself. Though maybe…" She shook her head again, frowning, and hugged her arms as if she was cold. "I had a touch of flu a few days ago. Guess I'm not as back to par as I'd thought. Boys!" she called, turning and starting for the jungle gym. "Time to go in. Carson, quit pretending you don't hear me. Zach—"

She stopped speaking. Stopped moving. And crumpled to the ground.

The fence was only four and a half feet high. I vaulted it and hit the ground running.

"Mrs. B...." She'd landed all crumpled, half on her side, with her face down. I turned her over gently, my heart pounding. The whites of her eyes showed. Her skin looked gray. I bent, putting my cheek near her mouth.

She wasn't breathing.

"Dad? Dad, what's wrong with Mrs. Bradshaw?"

Zach had vaulted off the jungle gym nearly as fast as I'd crossed over the fence. He stood nearby, the twins behind him, all of them looking scared.

"She's sick," I said, grabbing Zach. "Real sick." I rushed to the fence and dropped my son down on the other side. "Zach, go get Seely. She'll know what to do. She's upstairs. Go!"

He blinked once and took off.

I raced back to the unconscious woman, dropping to my knees beside her. Every year I refreshed my CPR training— but oh, God, I'd never had to use it. I took a deep breath and made myself sound calm. "Carson."

"Y-yes, sir?"

"Go in the house and call 911. Just push those three numbers—nine, one, one. Tell them we need an ambulance. You can do that, right?"

He nodded and pelted for the back door, his brother behind him.

A is for airway, B for breathing... I needed to make sure the airway was clear. I tilted Mrs. B.'s head back and pulled her jaw down. Her tongue wasn't blocking her airway. And I couldn't feel any breath on my hand.

I took a deep breath, pinched her nostrils shut, sealed her

mouth with mine and pushed air into her lungs. Did it again, paused—no change. She still wasn't breathing on her own.

Okay, C was for chest compressions. Fifteen of them, a little faster than one per second. I put one hand on top of the other right smack between her breasts, and pushed.

The chest should compress between an inch and a half and two inches. I tried to call up the kinesthetic memory of how it had felt to push on the dummy this way, praying I was using enough force, but not too much. I was terrified of breaking something. The instructor had told us that happens sometimes, that a strong man can crack a rib performing CPR. But she'd also said that a cracked rib is better than a stopped heart.

Mrs. B. was so small and so still. So horribly still.

…thirteen. Fourteen. Fifteen. Time for breaths again.

I'd finished two cycles and was on chest compressions again when Mrs. B.'s back door slammed open. James ran out. "They said they're coming. They're coming, Mr. McClain. Carson's still talking to them 'cause they told him to stay on the phone."

"Good." Fourteen. Fifteen.

"Is she gonna be okay? They'll make her okay, won't they?"

"I hope so." Time for breaths. I pinched her nose and bent.

"Go in the house, James," Seely called from the other side of the fence as I resumed chest compressions. "Your brother needs you to help him stay calm." I heard her climb over, but didn't look up. A moment later I saw her stocking-clad feet on the other side of Mrs. B. She dropped to her knees.

But she didn't get in position to take over the breath part. Instead she put her hands on either side of Mrs. B's neck right below the ears.

I finished the compressions and looked at Seely.

"It's bad, Ben," she said quietly. "Very bad." She bit her lip. "Will you trust me?"

"Yes."

"Then back away and don't let anyone touch her until I'm finished. Not for any reason."

Back away? Stop CPR? I hesitated. Surrendering control didn't come easily for me, and stopping CPR flew in the face of all reason.

But this was Seely. I nodded and pushed to my feet. My knee twinged sharply.

Seely put both hands on Mrs. B.'s chest, her expression calm and somehow distant. Focussed. It was the sort of expression you might see on an artist's face, or a nun at her prayers. "Oh," she said without looking up. "One more thing. If I pass out, don't let them take me to the hospital."

I took one quick, involuntary step toward her but made myself stop. Slowly, so gradually there was no way to draw a line and say when it happened, she began to glow.

Thirteen

The curtains were open at my bedroom window, but the glass gave back nothing except darkness and ghosts, vague reflections from a dimly lit room. Behind me, only one lamp was on—the pretty china one that had belonged to my mother.

It sat next to the bed where Seely slept. Doofus was asleep, too, belly-up on the rug by the bed. The pup had kept me company at first, but it was late.

Seely had been asleep or unconscious for almost seven hours.

Aside from Doofus, she and I were alone. Zach was back home with Gwen, Duncan was on patrol and Mrs. Bradshaw—

"Ben?"

I spun around, a grin breaking out. "You're back." I limped to the bed and sat next to her. "Thank God. I'm a patient man, but waiting for you to wake up…" I shook my head. "How do you feel?"

"Tired." She blinked up at me from the pile of pillows I'd arranged for her. "You were limping just now."

"I probably wasn't supposed to jump fences yet." She looked tired, all her abundant energy drained out, leaving her pale and too still. I smoothed her hair back.

"You probably weren't supposed to carry me up the stairs, either."

"Duncan did that. He came to pick up Zach this time, not Gwen." I'd had a heck of a time convincing him—and the paramedics—that Seely often fainted and didn't need to go to the hospital, too. Finally I'd asked him just to trust me, and never mind whether it made sense. After one of his long, silent moments, he'd agreed.

"Mrs. Bradshaw?"

"Doing well, last I heard. Her son and daughter-in-law are already at the hospital, and her other kids are on their way. Dr. Harry Meckle is baffled all over again. You okay?"

"Getting there." She glanced around. "How late is it?"

"About eleven-thirty."

Her eyebrows came to life, lifting slightly. "I would have expected you to panic long before this."

"I did. I called your mother."

"My…" She was speechless.

"That reminds me." I twisted around, reaching for a can of soda in the cooler I'd parked beside the bed hours ago. "She said to pour calories down you when you woke up."

"What do you mean, you called my mother?"

"Three times. She's in Directory Assistance," I pointed out, popping the top on the cola and filling a glass. "Nice lady. Different, but nice. I think she likes me. Here."

She took the glass but didn't seem to know what to do with it. "Daisy reassured you? You didn't worry?"

"Oh, I worried." The weight of all those hours returned, pressing down on me. "Daisy was straight with me about the danger. She told me to keep checking your breathing, make sure it didn't slow too much. If it had…" I swallowed. "If it had, I was to get you to the E.R. as fast as possible."

Seely touched my hand. "I really am okay, Ben. There's…kind of an edge. After a couple of bad experiences, I learned how to keep track of that edge so I don't fall over it."

I nodded, unable to speak for a moment, and gestured at her glass.

Her lips quirked. Obediently she sipped.

"I've got a sandwich and some of that cake you made yesterday, when you're ready to eat. Candy, too, if you want to take your calories straight."

"You really did talk to my mother."

"If I hadn't, you'd be in the hospital now. I didn't know enough to make the right decision on my own." I paused. "She told me a few other things, too. For example, she said you don't pass out and stay out this way unless the healing was especially hard. Unless the person was close to dying. Mrs. B. would have died if you hadn't been there, wouldn't she?"

"I don't know. There was severe damage, but they can sometimes restart a heart by shocking it. I…my best guess was that she wouldn't have made it."

I nodded thoughtfully. "You passed out after healing me. I was dying when you found me, wasn't I? I *would* have died if you hadn't done whatever you do."

She hesitated, then nodded.

I felt deep satisfaction. I hadn't imagined it. My memories of that time might be blurry and disjointed, but I hadn't imagined any of it. "So what is it you do?"

"Is this an ambush, Ben? Catch me while I'm weak and pry answers out of me?"

"Yeah, you could call it that. But I think I deserve a few explanations, don't you?"

There was a tired, defeated look in her eyes I didn't like, but I didn't see any way to get rid of it except the one I'd chosen. Finally she said, "Yes, I suppose you do. But I'd like to eat first."

I retrieved the tray I'd prepared earlier. She scooted up in bed until she was sitting, and I put some more pillows behind her, then set the tray on the bed and tried to come up with some easy things to talk about while she ate.

I talked about Mrs. Bradshaw. I figured Seely had to be interested in the woman whose life she'd saved, and I wanted her to see how many people's lives were affected because that one, nosy old woman was still around. So I told her about Mrs. B.'s grown children, and some of the other kids she'd taken care of at one time or another. Including my sister and brothers.

She had some color back in her face by the time she finished the cake, but there was still a haunted look to her eyes. Maybe whatever she did when she healed always left her that way. I didn't know, but I meant to find out.

I handed her a few of the hard candies, removed the tray and refilled her glass. "Your mom said the, ah…your family gift takes different forms, but with you it's healing. Only your gift is a lot stronger than hers or your granny's."

"My mother seems to have done a lot of talking."

"We hit it off." By the third call, I'd mostly gotten used to her habit of knowing things before I said them.

A wisp of a smile touched her lips. "Did she tell you what her form of the gift is?"

"No, but I think it has something to do with her being one hell of a good guesser."

That made her grin. It was there and gone quickly, but it was a grin. "Something like that. I guess you want me to tell you how it works. The truth is, I don't know myself. I've read some of the same books you've been reading because I'd like to understand, too. What did you think about that one?" She gestured at the book on top of the pile.

"It seemed pretty fact based," I said cautiously. "Less pseudoscience than some of them." The book was an account of a handful of well-documented cases and several anecdotal ones where the laying on of hands had apparently facilitated healing. It mentioned a study about prayer improving the chances of cardiac surgery patients, and suggested a connection.

"I thought so, too. Was anyone mentioned in that book able to do what I can?"

"It didn't sound like it."

"No. I've never found anyone else who can."

That sounded lonely. Isolating. "You've been doing this all your life?"

"It started when I was five. Little things at first—a scratch or bruise, a stomach bug. As I got older, I got stronger, until…" She shook her head, dismissing whatever she'd been about to say.

"You must have figured a few things out."

"You aren't going to let any of your questions go, are you?" She brought her knees up, wrapping her arms around them. "Okay, here's the short course. Healing 101. From what I can tell, I help the body do what it already knows how to do. I'm hell on wheels when it comes to healing wounds. Heart disease is harder, probably because I haven't had as much practice with it. But it's still a matter of helping the body heal."

She told me that she'd tried once to find out more about how her gift worked. While working as a paramedic, she'd healed a man who turned out to be a medical researcher with a Ph.D. He'd persuaded her to submit to tests.

And her gift had gone into hiding. "I couldn't heal a hangnail," she said wryly. "At first he thought I wasn't cooperating or was unconsciously blocking it. Maybe I was. We—the women in my family—have always had to hide what we were, so I've got a lot of conditioning about that. Or maybe, like Granny says, it's a God thing."

"What do you mean?"

"She thinks we aren't supposed to speak of our gift because God wants it that way." Seely shrugged. "I don't know. It was awful, though, when I didn't know if the gift would come back. Eventually Dr. Emerson convinced himself he'd imagined the whole thing, and I was a charlatan. It was spooky, watching him rewrite the past until he had a reality he could live with."

It had also been one more reason not to trust anyone with her secret. "You said you burned out as a paramedic. Too many hurt people to heal?"

She ducked her head, letting her hair hide her face. "Something like that."

I thought about what she'd said…and what she hadn't said. "There are limits on what you can do. You can't heal everything. That would be rough, thinking you should be able to save people and failing."

"Oh," she said, "you did it again…sometimes the body itself is confused. Autoimmune diseases, for example, seem to be beyond me. I can ease the symptoms of arthritis, but I can't cure it." She lifted her head and looked at me straightly. "I'm not much good with cancer, either."

My breath sighed out. So much for that faint, unvoiced hope. "It doesn't matter. Gwen's cancer is gone," I told her firmly. A thought struck. "Isn't it? Can you—"

"As far as I can tell, she's fine. I'm not a diagnostician," she warned me. "It isn't like on *Star Trek,* either. That empath who healed people by taking on their pain? It doesn't work that way."

"Thank God for that. So you don't, uh, feel what the people around you are feeling?"

"No. That would be horrible. I have to focus, to…reach out. And I have to be touching the person."

I nodded. She'd told me a lot I'd wanted to know, but she hadn't broached the important stuff. Maybe she didn't think I'd consider it important. "Something else Daisy told me about."

Seely looked down, picking at the wrapping on one of the butterscotch candies. "What?"

"She said that twit you used to live with—"

She broke into laughter. "'Twit.' God forgive me for being shallow, but I like that."

"*Bastard* seems like too important a word for him. Daisy said he talked a lot about how wonderful your gift was, seemed to accept it just fine. Until he actually saw you heal someone, and then he freaked. Things were never the same between you after that."

"That about sums it up, yes."

I said gently, "You're waiting for me to freak, aren't you?"

A spasm of emotion crossed her face. "Are you claiming you aren't already freaked? For God's sake, Ben, I know how you feel about psychic stuff!" She thumped me in the chest. "You choke on the word witch. Tell me you don't think my so-called gift is weird!"

"Hey." I caught her hand in mine. "Of course it is. But there are people called idiot savants. Some of them can't learn how to cross the street safely, but they can multiply four-digit numbers in their heads instantly. That's weird, too."

Her mouth twitched. "You calling me an idiot?"

"I'm calling you a woman with an ability that, yeah, is pretty damned strange. But it's a lot more useful than multiplying four-digit numbers in your head." I paused. "Of course, I'm hoping you'll tell me it doesn't have anything to do with chakras and auras."

"Well, I've never seen an aura—"

"Thank God."

"But chakras do seem to be a pretty accurate description of the way energy moves through the body. I don't see that energy, but I feel it."

I sighed. "I'll adjust."

Her smile flickered. She went back to messing with the candy wrapper—not removing it, just twisting and untwisting the cellophane. "You're handling all this better than I thought you would. But you haven't thought about the ramifications."

I snorted. "I've chased my brain in circles for over a week, trying to think out the ramifications. I read about chakras, for God's sake. If I haven't got it all figured out, well, you haven't given me much to work on until now."

"So think some more," she urged me softly without looking up. "If I can start a heart beating again, I could stop one, too. Doesn't that worry you? You've been sleeping next to a woman who could stop your heart in your sleep."

"If that's what the twit was worried about, I may have to upgrade him to bastard after all."

She gave the wrapper another twist. "He had reason."

"Now you're being stupid. Any woman could murder the

man sleeping next to her, if she's so inclined. Poison, a gun, a knife between the ribs—just because you could do it in a weird way doesn't mean you would."

All of a sudden she looked up, trapping me with those haunted eyes. "There's one big difference between me and all your hypothetical murderesses. I've done it. When I was eight years old, I stopped my grandfather's heart."

Shock hit, stealing my breath. Rage followed close on its heels.

"What did he do to you?" I demanded, seizing her shoulders. "What did that—that—" I couldn't think of a word bad enough. "What did he do to force you to defend yourself that way?"

"He—I—why did you ask that?" She was staring, her eyes as big as mine must have been when she healed Mrs. B. "How did you know?"

"Aw, sweetheart. How can you even ask?" Rage drained out, leaving an ache behind. I reached for her, turning her so she settled against my chest instead of the pillows, and sighed. "I don't know if this helps you any, but I feel better."

I could see enough of the curve of her cheek to know that she smiled. "You're a good man, Ben."

"Damn straight, I am." Her answering chuckle sounded damp, but real. I stroked her hair. "He must have done something terrible, something that frightened you badly."

"Yes." She hesitated. "You've already guessed, haven't you? He tried to molest me. To…feel me up, at least. I don't know how far he would have gone."

"You were *eight*," I said, sick and baffled. "You were only eight."

"It's why my grandmother hates me, of course. She refused to believe the judge could have done anything like that."

I thought about that for a moment. "He didn't die."

"No, I…once I realized what I'd done, I kept him alive until help arrived. I didn't know how to heal the damage, though. Not then." She shuddered. "It was horrible, having to touch him to keep his heart beating. But what I'd done was worse. I hadn't known…he'd exposed himself, you see. When he tried to make m-me…anyway, I screamed at him to stop. I screamed it with everything in me. I wasn't thinking about stopping his heart, but that's what I did."

I couldn't speak. I could only hold her and pet her and try to be glad for her sake that she hadn't killed the bastard.

After a while she straightened. Her eyes were moist, but she smiled. "You mustn't be picturing me as horribly traumatized. Daisy wouldn't permit that. My father sent me home to her after it happened…he wouldn't talk to me about it, but Daisy did. She helped me sort things out so that I didn't blame myself, or feel smirched."

Maybe she didn't blame herself for the way a sick old man had tried to molest her, but she was carrying a load of hurt over having defended herself the only way she could. I didn't know what to do about that. I rubbed my knuckles across her cheek, wiping away the dampness. "I knew I liked your mother."

"I like her myself."

She still looked tired, but the haunted look was gone. There was a shy sort of happiness in her eyes instead. "So." I cleared my throat. "No more big, shocking secrets to reveal?"

"That was about it," she agreed gravely.

"How'd I do? Did I pass?"

"Ben, I wasn't testing you. I wouldn't…oh, all right," she said before I could interrupt, her smile spreading slowly in the way I loved. "You passed with flying colors."

"Then maybe you'll agree to marry me." Even as her eyes

rounded I cursed myself. "Hell. I didn't mean to blurt it out that way." But I couldn't help smiling. "That's the second time I've made you speechless tonight. Must be a record."

"I think it is," she agreed faintly. "Ben, we talked about—we said we wouldn't—"

"I know you didn't want this to turn into anything serious." I captured her hands and held them between us. "But think about it. We're good together, in bed and out. Good for each other, I think. I'm not good with words," I said gruffly, "but I think you're special. Incredibly special. I'm not talking about your gift, but about…well, you. All of you."

Her eyes were getting damp again. I didn't know if that was good or bad, so I rushed forward, hoping to convince her. "I think about you when you're not around. I think about how it might be with us twenty years from now, too. And about how beautiful you'd look growing round with my child. You're great with Zach. You'd make a wonderful mother."

She jerked, nearly pulling her hands out of mine. "Ben—"

"I wouldn't be marrying you to give Zach a mother," I said quickly. "That's not what I mean. He's got a mom already. I mean—aw, hell, you're crying. Don't do that. Don't cry, Seely."

But the tears spilled over anyway. "B-Ben, I can't have children. I told you that, right at the start."

For a moment I just stared at her. Then, carefully, as if I were threading a path lined with land mines, I said, "You meant that you were on the pill."

But she was shaking her head. "I meant exactly what I said. You didn't need to use protection because I can't catch or transmit venereal diseases. And I can't get pregnant."

I dropped her hands. In the whited-out blankness of my brain, thoughts began to whirl. She'd said she didn't have any more shocking secrets, but she hadn't thought this was a secret. She'd thought I knew. That I accepted… I shook my head. "You can't be sure. Unless you've had some kind of accident or surgery—and you could fix that sort of thing, couldn't you? You could heal it."

"I tried to get pregnant, Ben. Me a-and the twit." Her smile wobbled and broke. "We both wanted a child, and we tried for years. We were both tested and the doctors didn't find anything wrong, but—"

"Then maybe there isn't anything wrong. Maybe his sperm just weren't compatible with you somehow." Hadn't I read about that sort of thing somewhere?

"It's my gift." Her voice was bitter. "The women in my family aren't very fertile. My mother had only one child. So did my grandmother and my great-grandmother. Supposedly, the gift is stronger in me than in any of them. It…maybe it 'heals' a pregnancy before it can get started. Maybe it kills the sperm as soon as they hit my womb, just as it kills viruses that enter my bloodstream. I don't know." The shrug of her shoulders was infinitely weary. "And I don't suppose it matters."

"Of course it matters." I scrubbed a hand over my hair, but that wasn't enough to quiet the screaming jitters making a mess of my insides. I pushed off the bed and began to pace. "Maybe you're wrong about your gift doing it. Maybe it's incompatible sperm."

"Steven wasn't my only lover. And I've never used birth control."

What was it about me that I had only to reach out, try to touch a dream, to have it turn to dust? "Maybe there's some way to control it. You must be able to control your gift most of the time."

"I control whether I reach out with it or not, but the gift— oh, we don't have words for this!"

"Try. Please try." Maybe she was too close to the problem. Maybe I'd be able to see something she'd missed, if only I could understand how her gift worked.

She sighed, shoved back her hair and tried. "In my own body, the gift is sort of on autopilot. It heals me automatically. When I heal someone else, I impose…call it a template, the template from my own energy field. That's why I told you not to let anyone touch Mrs. Bradshaw while I was working on her. Another person's touch interferes with the template. Once someone's body accepts my template, it knows how to heal quickly. I help that healing along, but it's like—oh, like pushing a wagon as opposed to steering it."

"Is there any way to, uh—to adjust the template?"

She shook her head. "Tampering could destroy it. Maybe me, too. I could develop cancer or some degenerative condition."

"No. God, no." I stopped, hands clenched.

"This is why I said our relationship needed to be temporary." She laughed once, mirthlessly. "Though you can be forgiven for thinking I didn't mean it, because I didn't. But if ever a man needed to have children, it's you. I knew you were in the market for marriage, but I kept hoping—"

"Wait a minute. How did you know that?"

She looked at me, a wry twist to her mouth. "One of the things I love about you is your honesty. You don't hide what you're thinking or feeling very well, even if sometimes you might like to."

One of the things she loved? My heart gave a little jump. I told myself firmly that it's possible to love some things about a person without being in love. But still…

I rubbed my chest as if I could calm a jumpy heart that way. "Okay, maybe I have been giving marriage some thought lately. That doesn't mean…" But marriage *did* mean kids to me. In my mind, in my heart, marriage and children were so intertwined I didn't know how to think of one without the other. "I have to think about this. I need a little time to think things out."

"You'll have plenty of time to do that."

Something in her voice dragged my attention away from the turmoil within. "I'm an idiot. This was no time to hit you with everything, when you're exhausted from helping Mrs. B." I went to the bed, sat down and patted her hand. "You lie down. I'll get rid of the tray and be right back. We'll work things out," I said firmly. "But in the morning, not now when we're both tired."

I was talking too much and too fast, trying to sound positive when I felt anything but. Seely was right. I wasn't good at pretending. I hadn't had much practice.

I wasn't used to running away, either, but that's what it felt like when I carried the tray down to the darkened kitchen. I took my time putting things away. And when I returned to the bedroom and found her asleep, I was relieved.

I was also genuinely wiped out, though, so maybe that was excusable. Waiting for Seely to wake up had been rough. Nothing that had happened since she did had been exactly easy, either. I closed the curtains, stripped and climbed in beside her, close enough to drape an arm over her. Tomorrow, I promised myself. Tomorrow I'd sort things out. But the ghostly sound of dreams crumbling made a dismal music to carry with me into sleep.

In the morning Seely told me she was leaving.

Fourteen

"What do you mean, you're moving out?" I growled. I was sitting up in bed. Seely was bustling around the room, removing things that hadn't been there very long.

I'd woken up to the sound of her pulling her suitcase out of the closet. Not a good way to start the day.

"Just what I said." She opened another drawer. "You need some time to think about things. Well, so do I."

"One big difference." I threw back the covers, climbed out of bed and stalked over to her. "I wasn't going to kick you out while I did my thinking."

"Oh, Ben." She stopped and looked at me, and her face was so sad it made me feel even worse. "I'm sorry. I know this is sudden. But I've done everything suddenly with you, from going to bed together to agreeing to live together."

"Those were good ideas. This is a mistake. A huge mistake."

"What's one more mistake? I've already made such a mess

of things. I thought—hoped—oh, I hoped far too many things. And without much reason," she added bitterly. "It isn't as if you led me on." She tossed a stack of T-shirts into her over-size suitcase.

"No, I just proposed to you. Dammit, quit that." I grabbed her shirts and stuck them back in the drawer. "You're overre-acting. This whole relationship bit is about working things out. How can we work anything out if we aren't together?"

"I'll overreact if I want to!" She snatched up the T-shirts and crammed them into the suitcase. "Oh," she said, closing her eyes. "Just listen to me. I sound about five years old."

"You need some food in your system. Coffee. Get your blood sugar stabilized, and things won't look so—so however they look that makes you think you have to do this."

She shook her head. Her eyes were just about drowning in sadness, but her mouth was set in a stubborn line. She reached for the next drawer.

I pushed her hand away from it. "Tell me why," I said. Or maybe I was begging by then. I was beginning to feel desper-ate, and I didn't like it. "The least you can do is tell me why you're leaving."

She flicked me a glance. "You don't want an explanation. You want an excuse to argue me out of it."

"Don't I deserve a chance to do that?" My voice was get-ting louder.

"Okay. Yes. Oh, damn," she said as her eyes filled. Angrily she dashed her hand across them. "I promised myself I wouldn't cry. Here's the deal, Ben." She met my eyes. Hers were shiny with the tears she refused to shed. "I'm not as hon-est as you are. I went into this saying one thing, but hoping for something else. I...I hoped you'd grow to care for me."

"It worked."

"Which is why it was so wrong of me. Oh, don't you see?" She took two jerky paces and whirled to face me again. "I went after you with both barrels. I wanted you, and I persuaded myself I could have you, that you wouldn't be hurt."

"So now that you've got me, you want to throw me back?"

"I thought you knew!" she cried. "I thought you knew I couldn't have children, that you were okay with it. But that was my fault, too—that you misunderstood. I was so busy protecting myself. I didn't tell you about my gift. I didn't explain."

"If you're leaving in order to save me from myself," I growled, "don't."

"I'm not. At least, not entirely. I'm still protecting myself. I don't know what to do. I thought I could handle whatever happened, but…" She hugged her arms around herself as if she were cold. "I'm already hurting. I don't want to be hurt more."

Another kind of pain blended with the unholy mix churning in my gut. "I wouldn't hurt you, Seely. You have to know that."

"No?" For the first time, her eyebrows had a comment to make, lifting incredulously. "Tell me you still want to marry me, Ben. That it wouldn't wreck your dreams if you never had more children. That you wouldn't come to regret it—and resent me."

I wanted to say that. I *wanted* to. But… "Dammit, I need a little time to get used to the idea. From what you said, you've had years to grow accustomed to it."

"I'm going to give you time. And while you're getting your head straight, I'm going to do the same."

"But…" I rubbed a hand over my face. I wasn't going to beg, dammit. I took a deep breath and let it out slowly. "You believe you have to leave to do that."

"I do." Her chin went up another notch. "Maybe I'm wrong. Tell me one more thing. Are you still in love with Gwen?"

My mouth opened—and closed again.

She nodded slowly. "That's what I thought." She turned back to the bureau, yanked a drawer open and pulled out some jeans. They went in the suitcase. She zipped it shut.

"You aren't giving me a chance! You hit me with that question out of the blue, when I didn't have a clue you even suspected…. Dammit, how do I know? I'm feeling *everything* right now! Everything all at once!"

"Me, too," she whispered, and jerked the suitcase upright. "I'd like you to promise me that you won't call me or come around, not until I contact you."

I was shaking my head before she finished. "Forget it."

"I know you, you see." Her smile made a brief appearance, dying on a tremble of her bottom lip. "Once you've set your sights on a goal, you're as likely to turn aside as an avalanche. Look at the way you kept crawling up that mountain, when anyone else would have given up and died." Again her smile flickered—fast and uneasy, so unlike her usual molasses smiles. "It's rather awe-inspiring to be the target of all that determination. But I can't handle it right now."

I was breathing fast, as if I'd been running uphill. I forced myself to take a breath and hold it. I had to stay calm. Stay in control. We couldn't both panic at the same time—and that's what she was doing, whatever she said. "You've got money coming to you. I need to know where you'll be staying so I can send it on."

"I'll give you my address when you give me your promise. If you won't promise, I'll leave Highpoint. I'll vanish. I can do it. I'd rather not, but I will if I have to."

So I promised. It was like chewing on ground glass, but I promised. "You will call," I told her. "You said you'd call."

She nodded.

I let her carry that big, heavy suitcase downstairs herself. I didn't go with her. I stood in my bedroom and tried to make my breathing work right and listened as the suitcase thumped down those stairs behind her. Listened as the front door opened. And closed.

Then I spun around, grabbed the first thing I saw and hurled it against the wall. And stood there in among the shards of my mother's pretty china lamp, stood there and kept breathing, surrounded by thousands of unmendable pieces.

Four days later, I was returning to the office from the Patterson site. It was about six o'clock. Dr. Harold Meckle pulled into the parking lot just before I did, and the jerk took my parking place.

"Mr. McClain," he called as he got out of his shiny Lincoln. "I need to talk to you."

I was not in a good mood. I hadn't even wanted to be around my family since Seely walked out. I sure didn't have the patience for Harry. "I'm busy right now." I slammed the truck door.

"This will just take a moment. I'd like to examine you." Harry's eyes glittered with excitement. "I'm on to something. Something big."

"Yeah? I think you're just on something."

"It's that woman. I know it is." He followed me to the office door. "I don't know what she does, but I mean to find out. I understand the two of you have broken up. I had hoped you would persuade her to speak with me, but perhaps that wouldn't be feasible."

I snorted. "Since she isn't talking to me—yeah, that's a good assumption." I stuck my key in the office door.

"I treated Mrs. Bradshaw when she arrived at the E.R., you

know. She had a major heart attack, yet there is no cardiac damage."

"Go away, Harry." I opened the door.

"I can't put together a paper without solid facts. I have to examine you. You're using that shoulder normally. That shouldn't be possible."

"Consider the possibility that you've made a mistake," I said, stepping inside. "A big one."

He was still jabbering when I shut the door in his face.

I sat at my desk without turning on the light. I didn't really have any work I couldn't do at home, but I wouldn't go there until I had to. As hard as it can be to face an empty house, one filled with might-have-beens is worse.

I thought about Harry, who wanted to write a paper and get famous, and never mind the consequences to the human lab rat he proposed to write about. That made me think about Seely, of course, but there was nothing new about that. I hadn't had a moment free of her since she left me.

The worst of it was that stupid promise she'd pulled out of me. Lord! I leaned back in my chair, staring at the ceiling. How had I let myself be maneuvered into such a miserable position? If I could just go to her, talk to her…

And tell her what? I was still torn up about not having children. I hated knowing I'd never get to meet the curly-haired little girl I'd imagined swinging in the backyard. Dammit, did Seely expect me to be happy about that?

I knew where she was. She'd sent a polite little note giving me her address—a cheap, rent-by-the-week motel on the edge of town. I'd mailed her paycheck to her, but my damned promise kept me from doing anything else. I couldn't even let her know Harry was determined to make trouble for her.

Wait a minute. I couldn't contact *her*…but I hadn't promised anything about her family.

Seely's brother, Jonathan, I'd learned, was on the hospital board.

Paper crinkled as I bent and retrieved the phone book. Her stupid, polite little note was in my shirt pocket because I couldn't stand to put it away.

Jonathan Burns might be a decent sort, or he might take after his grandmother. Either way, I figured he had an interest in seeing that Dr. Harold Meckle didn't turn Seely into some sort of medical tabloid star. Maybe Jonathan would worry about what that would do to her. Maybe he'd just be worried about the consequences for the rest of his precious family.

Not that Seely would threaten to divulge what her grandfather had done, but I had no such compunctions. Besides, she still had those issues. She needed to find out if she liked her brother or never wanted to see him again.

I reached for the phone.

Seely had been gone a full week when I pulled into another parking lot. This time I was in a taxi, though. And the parking lot belonged to the Wagonwheel bar.

I'm not much for what the younger crowd calls clubbing. If I want to play pool, I go to Binton's. If I want to dance, I go to the resort. Tonight I wasn't interested in pool or dancing. I wanted to honor an old tradition and try to drink a woman out of my mind.

Not that I thought it would work, but a desperate man will try anything.

The Wagonwheel was the right spot for serious drinking. It wasn't a dive, but it wasn't fancy, either. At eight o'clock on a Thursday night the place was busy but not packed. I passed a few people I knew on my way to the bar, including a couple of men from Manny's crew. I nodded but didn't pause. I wasn't here to socialize.

I'd ordered a double bourbon when someone slapped me on the back. "Hey, there, Ben! Haven't seen you around lately."

I turned my head and grimaced. Chuck Meyers is a big, bluff, party-loving kind of guy who'd played football with me back in high school. He's one reason I don't spend much time in bars. Too easy to run into men like him. "I've been busy recuperating."

"That's your story and you're stickin' to it, huh?" He chuckled. "Don't guess it had a thing to do with that sexy nurse of yours. Saw her when I went to get my kid's school records the other day. Whew. Hot stuff." He shook his hand as if it had been singed.

"Shut up, Chuck."

"Hey, I saw her, too." That came from the man on the other side of Chuck, a scrawny little runt with a mustache. I recognized him vaguely from the hospital—he was an orderly or something. "She was at that Chinese place on Elm with this good-looking blond dude." He gave me a bleary grin. "Tough luck, McClain. Got to bite to lose one like that."

Now that was just what I needed to hear. I turned away, doing my best to ignore the two men. Seely hadn't called me. No, she'd decided to go out with some blond guy instead of working out our problems.

My drink arrived. I told the bartender to run me a tab and got my first swallow down. But Chuck and his buddy were hard to ignore. They were talking about Seely.

"Man, what I wouldn't give to have just one little taste of that," the scrawny one said.

"Some men don't know when they're lucky. Not that I'd want to stop with one taste, myself. Did you get a look at those tits?"

I sighed. "Chuck, I told you to shut up."

"I'm talkin' to Bill, here," he told me. "Since you're so unfriendly tonight."

"Well, you won't be talking about Seely anymore. To Bill or anyone else. Got it?"

"Don't see how that's any of your business. Can't blame you for being touchy, though." He slapped me on the back again, grinning. "Be strange if you weren't out of sorts after losing that piece of ass. And oh, man, those tits!" He made grabbing, squeezing motions in the air.

So I hit him.

Fifteen

There's something particularly humiliating about almost being arrested by your little brother.

"Watch your head," Duncan said.

I stopped dead beside his patrol car. "If you think I'm going to ride in the cage in back, I'll have to report you for drinking on duty."

One side of his mouth kicked up. "Guess I can let you ride up front. Though I may rethink using the handcuffs. Transporting a suspect who isn't properly restrained is against regs."

I growled and jerked open the passenger-side door. He was enjoying this entirely too much.

Duncan grinned and rounded the back of the car, got in on his side and started the engine. "I can't get over you starting a brawl in a bar. What were you thinking?"

"I didn't start a fight. I hit one man one time." Once, I

thought with satisfaction, had been all it took. Chuck had dropped like a felled tree.

"I guess those other three fellows just imagined they were in a fight."

"Some people are too suggestible."

He sighed and pulled out of the lot. It sounded a lot like the sighs I used to heave when he was a teenager. "So why did you hit Meyers?"

"The other guy was too much of a runt. Chuck is more my size."

"That isn't quite what I meant."

I knew that, of course. I gave it a couple moments, then said, "They talked about Seely in a way I couldn't stomach. About her body, really. It wasn't about her at all, just what they wanted to do with her body. I warned Chuck. He wouldn't quit."

"As a man, I understand. As your brother, I sympathize. As a cop, I ought to be reading you your rights."

"No one pressed charges." Thanks in part to my promise to pay the owner for damages, even though I hadn't broken anything. Not even Chuck's jaw, since I'd had the sense to aim for his belly. You can break your hand hitting someone in the jaw.

"Drunk and disorderly."

"I'm not drunk, dammit! I only had time for one swallow." But Duncan was grinning again, so I knew he'd just been yanking my chain.

Neither of us said anything for a few blocks. I was thinking about how pathetic it was when a man couldn't even manage to get drunk without causing all sorts of ruckus when Duncan spoke again. "I'm sorry things didn't work out for you and Seely."

"Yeah. Me, too."

"Gwen has spoken with her a couple of times since she moved out."

I was surprised, though maybe I shouldn't have been. They'd hit it off pretty well. "That's good, I guess."

"Seely wouldn't tell her what went wrong." Duncan paused. "Gwen is afraid maybe *she's* what went wrong."

"No! Tell her…" I scrubbed my face with my hand, sighed and got it said. "I had feelings for Gwen at one time. You know that. But that's in the past." Something I hadn't made clear to Seely—but she hadn't given me much of a chance, springing it on me that way.

Or maybe I hadn't made it clear because it hadn't been clear to me, either. But I was beginning to see a lot of things I'd never managed to bring into focus before. Losing Seely was a lot like dying cold and alone on a mountain. It clarified things. "Tell Gwen that the problem is me. Not her, and not Seely." I sighed. "I found out she can't have children, and I didn't handle it well."

"It isn't easy when the woman you love isn't able to bear your child."

There was an edge to his voice—not much, just a hint. And all of a sudden I knew myself for a fool.

The type of cancer Gwen had been treated for made pregnancy dangerous. It was likely that the only child she'd ever have was Zach…*my* son. I'd felt sorry for myself often enough because Zach wasn't wholly mine, living with me. But Zach was also probably the only son Duncan would ever have.

I'd never thought about what that must mean to him. And he'd never spoken about it. Duncan was the kind of quiet hero whose sacrifices were easy to overlook.

And me…I was ashamed. "You'd know about that, wouldn't you?" I said at last, as we turned off on my street.

Duncan didn't say anything until we pulled up in the drive behind my truck. Then he turned to me. "If you love Seely, you'll grieve with her for what you can't have. And it won't be just *your* unborn children you mourn. It will be hers, too."

A few more things became clear. Painfully so. After a moment I managed to say, "How did you turn into more of an adult than me, when I had such a big head start?"

He grinned, a subtle flash in the darkness. "I had a great example. Someone who raised kids he didn't father."

I nodded. "Frank McDonald, maybe? He's great with his stepkids."

"No, you jerk. You."

The Sleep-Rite Inn wasn't much, a horseshoe-shaped cluster of rooms around a courtyard of cracked and pitted asphalt, with a perpetually empty swimming pool as the centerpiece. The blinking neon "Vac-n-y" sign pretty much summed the place up.

Number fourteen was two doors down from the highway. I was scowling as I knocked on the door.

"Go away," number fourteen's inhabitant called, "or I'll call the police."

"For God's sake, Seely, what kind of place did you pick to run away to that you have to call the cops if someone knocks on your door?"

The door was so thin I heard her gasp. A moment later the lock clicked and the door opened, and there she stood in one of her old sweatshirts and the bottom half to my pajamas, rolled up at the hems. After a moment she said, "You weren't knocking, you were pounding. And it's ten-thirty at night. What are you doing here?"

"Breaking my promise. Can I come in?"

Her face had that closed, wary look that I hated, but she stood aside. I went in.

I'd never been inside the Sleep-Rite Inn's rooms before. I looked around, my scowl deepening. "This is a dump. If you needed money, why didn't you say so? We could have called it a loan," I said grudgingly.

The tiniest smile flickered deep in her eyes. "You think I

should have borrowed money from you so I could live more comfortably when I left you?"

"Since you probably wouldn't let me give it to you, yeah."

"And you came here at ten-thirty to tell me so."

I flushed. I'd swung off course for a moment. "I came because that was a stupid promise. How can you get your head straight when you don't know if I've got mine straight yet?"

She tilted her head to one side. "Have you ever broken a promise before, Ben?"

I didn't think so. In fact, I was pretty damned sure I hadn't. I began to pace. "I had this all worked out, what I was going to say and how to say it. You're throwing me off."

"Sorry."

She didn't look sorry. "The thing is," I said, halting in front of her, "that I can change course. Change my mind, that is. It may take me a while, but I get there. We'll adopt. If you want to," I added when her expression didn't change. "A very smart man helped me see that kids don't have to start out being mine to end up that way."

"You still want to marry me, then."

It wasn't a question, but I thought I heard an ache behind it. "More than I've ever wanted anything in my life. Seely…" I wanted badly to touch her, but I didn't trust myself. Sex had been too easy for us. It had broken down some walls, maybe, but at the same time sex had made it easy to think we didn't have to talk, too.

Or maybe that part was just me. I swallowed. "I'm not good with words. And I'm stubborn. Sometimes that's good, but it means I can take a while to see the obvious. You asked about Gwen. Well, it's real obvious to me now that Gwen was a dream, part of how I thought life was supposed to go. What I didn't see was that sometimes you have to let go of the dream in order to take hold of reality."

Her eyes misted. "Ben…"

"Let me finish." Now I reached for her. I couldn't help it. I put my hands on her shoulders and ran them down her arms to her hands and held on. "You're my reality, Seely. And you're better than any dream I ever mooned over. There's more *of* you—more giving, more fun, more…I don't know how say it right. Just *more.* So if you need time, I'll give you time. If you want to go back to just dating, we can do that. Just don't shut me out. Please."

She threw herself at me. She was laughing, or maybe crying.

Or maybe that part was me, too. I blinked several times, stroking her hair, savoring the feeling of having her in my arms again. "So, you want to go out with me?"

"I want to marry you, you idiot." She raised her head, and yes, her eyes were shiny wet. And her smile was huge. "I always have. From the moment I found a man too stubborn to die crawling up a mountain…that's another family tradition, you see. Knowing it right away when we meet the love of our lives. But you still haven't said what you're supposed to."

I hunted frantically through the last few minutes, trying to think of exactly what I'd said. "Did I remember to ask you to marry me instead of telling you?"

She shook her head, but it was one of those fond, he's-only-a-man head shakes women use sometimes. "You're supposed to tell me you love me."

"I…" A second's pure panic hit when the words wouldn't come. "I don't think I've said that in a long time. Give me a second."

"How long has it been?" she asked gently.

Another memory search, but this one took longer, reaching back…years.

Could it really have been that long? Surely I'd said it sometime, to someone…but you didn't say stuff like that to your brothers. And Annie—well, she knew, so I'd never had to say it. I cleared my throat. "The last time I remember saying that was to my parents. They were about to get on their plane."

"And they never came back, did they?"

"But that's stupid. I got over that a long time ago. I…" Was still not saying the words she needed to hear. There was a buzzing in my ears. I felt almost sick. "Okay, I can do this. I…I love you."

The kiss she gave me then was guaranteed to erase any lingering trauma associated with those words. After a long moment she sighed and laid her head on my shoulder. "And I love you. I fell hard and fast, so fast it nearly scared me clear out of town. If Duncan hadn't found me at the bus station…"

My arms tightened around her. "I owe him." For more than one thing.

"I wanted to call you so many times. I hated leaving. But if you didn't love me, I couldn't marry you—not when I couldn't give you the children you craved. I was afraid I'd say yes, anyway," she admitted. "That's why I left."

"You could have told me you loved me," I pointed out.

"Sure. And then you'd have felt honor bound to marry me, even if you weren't in love."

I opened my mouth to argue…and shut it again. She might be right. I couldn't say for sure, since by the time she'd walked out I'd been head-over-heels for her, even if I was too dumb to know it.

Something occurred to me. "You mean you were going to take the bus because of me, not because of the deal with your brother?"

She nodded. "Partly. Mostly. Speaking of brothers…" She gave me another soft kiss. "Thank you. I had lunch with Jonathan yesterday, and he told me you'd spoken to him. He had a talk with Dr. Meckle—who, it seems, has lost all interest in writing a paper about such an uncooperative subject."

"That's great." I hugged her. So the blond guy she'd had lunch with had been her brother. That was a relief in more ways than one. Jonathan Burns had been pretty thrown by learning he had a sister, and I hadn't been sure he would follow up on my suggestion to contact her.

I decided she didn't need to know I'd jumped to an unfortunate conclusion about who she'd had lunch with. "What did you think of Jonathan?"

"I think…" She took a deep breath, let it out. "I liked him. It will take time to build a real relationship, of course—we'll have to see how things work out. He…seemed glad to meet me. And as unsure as I was about where we go from here."

It was a start. I was getting the idea that life wasn't one long, unfolding road, but a whole series of starts and stops and then starting up again—a little smarter each time, if you were lucky.

"Are you sure you don't mind?" She searched my face. "About not having children, that is. Unless we adopt, which I would like…but you have to be sure."

"Of course I mind. I can't think of anything sweeter than watching you grow big with my child, and I'm sad that we won't get to experience it." I smiled down at her tenderly. "But that's only one part of the deal, after all, and not the most important part."

A smile slid across her face, slow as sunrise…mischievous as a puppy. "Maybe it's just as well we can't mingle our gene pools. Who knows what the offspring of two strong psychics might be like?"

I snorted. "Only one person in this room is gifted in that way."

"Ben, I don't glow."

"Of course you do. I *saw* you. Twice."

"You must have seen my aura. No one else has ever seen me glow when I heal—not me, my mother or my granny. Not the people I healed. Not the researcher who decided I'd made it all up." When I just stared at her, she chuckled. "Ask Zach or Mrs. Bradshaw if you don't believe me, but think about it. How could I have kept my healing a secret all these years if I lit up like a Christmas tree every time?"

"You don't glow."

She shook her head.

I thought it over. "Okay, you don't glow to everyone else. Just to me. That doesn't mean I see auras. Otherwise I'd have been seeing them all over the place, and I haven't. Just with you." I smiled, and it came kind of slow and easy, too. "I trust what I see when I look at you, Seely."

What I saw was real, all right. Love is about as real as you can get.

Fourteen Months Later

An invitation addressed to Jonathan and Daniel Burns:

Benjamin and Seely McClain
hope you can attend a celebration on
Wednesday, July 29 at 7 p.m.
welcoming their son, Peter Liu McClain,
into his new home.

In lieu of gifts, donations may be sent to:
Adoption Alliance.
2121 S. Oneida St., Suite 420
Denver, CO 80224-2575 USA
Phone: 303-584-9900
Email: info@adoptall.com

* * * * *

*There's just one McClain bachelor left—
but who will be right for the Charming Charlie?
Stay tuned for more details!*

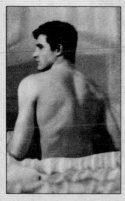

Silhouette Desire from *his* point of view.

BETWEEN DUTY AND DESIRE
by Leanne Banks
(Silhouette Desire #1599, on sale August 2004)

MEETING AT MIDNIGHT
by Eileen Wilks
(Silhouette Desire #1605, on sale September 2004)

LOST IN SENSATION
by Maureen Child
(Silhouette Desire #1611, on sale October 2004)

FOR SERVICES RENDERED
by Anne Marie Winston
(Silhouette Desire #1617, on sale November 2004)

Available at your favorite retail outlet.

If you enjoyed what you just read,
then we've got an offer you can't resist!

Take 2 bestselling
love stories FREE!

Plus get a FREE surprise gift!

Clip this page and mail it to Silhouette Reader Service™

IN U.S.A.	**IN CANADA**
3010 Walden Ave.	P.O. Box 609
P.O. Box 1867	Fort Erie, Ontario
Buffalo, N.Y. 14240-1867	L2A 5X3

YES! Please send me 2 free Silhouette Desire® novels and my free surprise gift. After receiving them, if I don't wish to receive anymore, I can return the shipping statement marked cancel. If I don't cancel, I will receive 6 brand-new novels every month, before they're available in stores! In the U.S.A., bill me at the bargain price of $3.80 plus 25¢ shipping and handling per book and applicable sales tax, if any*. In Canada, bill me at the bargain price of $4.47 plus 25¢ shipping and handling per book and applicable taxes**. That's the complete price and a savings of at least 10% off the cover prices—what a great deal! I understand that accepting the 2 free books and gift places me under no obligation ever to buy any books. I can always return a shipment and cancel at any time. Even if I never buy another book from Silhouette, the 2 free books and gift are mine to keep forever.

225 SDN DZ9F
326 SDN DZ9G

Name	(PLEASE PRINT)	
Address	Apt.#	
City	State/Prov.	Zip/Postal Code

Not valid to current Silhouette Desire® subscribers.

Want to try two free books from another series?
Call 1-800-873-8635 or visit www.morefreebooks.com.

* Terms and prices subject to change without notice. Sales tax applicable in N.Y.
** Canadian residents will be charged applicable provincial taxes and GST.
All orders subject to approval. Offer limited to one per household.
® are registered trademarks owned and used by the trademark owner and or its licensee.

DES04R   ©2004 Harlequin Enterprises Limited

COMING NEXT MONTH

#1609 THE LAWS OF PASSION—Linda Conrad
Dynasties: The Danforths
When attorney Marcus Danforth was falsely arrested, FBI agent
Dana Aldrich rushed to prove his innocence. Brought together by the
laws of the court, they discovered their intense mutual attraction ignited
the laws of passion. Yet Dana wanted more from this sizzling-hot lawyer—
she wanted love....

#1610 CAUGHT IN THE CROSSFIRE—Annette Broadrick
The Crenshaws of Texas
The arousing connection between blue-eyed Jared Crenshaw and
Lindsey Russell was undeniable from the moment they met. Before he
knew it, Jake had woken up in Lindsey's bed, but how had he gotten there?
He was certain they'd been caught in the crossfire of somebody's scandalous
scheme....

#1611 LOST IN SENSATION—Maureen Child
Mantalk
Dr. Sam Holden was still reeling from the past when Tricia Wright swept
him up into a whirlwind of passion. This woman was an intriguing force of
nature: blond, bubbly and hot as hell. But their joint future was put
permanently on hold until he could conquer the past that haunted him.

#1612 DARING THE DYNAMIC SHEIKH—Kristi Gold
The Royal Wager
Princess Raina Kahlil had no desire to marry the man she'd been promised
to. That was until she met Sheikh Dharr Ibn Halim face-to-dashingly-
handsome-face. While Raina found herself newly drawn to her culture and
country, she was even more intensely drawn to its future king....

#1613 VERY PRIVATE DUTY—Rochelle Alers
The Blackstones of Virginia
Federal agent Jeremy Blackstone was the only man Tricia Parker had ever
loved. Now, years after they'd parted, she was nursing him back to health.
Tricia struggled not to fall under Jeremy's sensual spell, but how could she
resist playing the part of both nurse *and* lover?

#1614 BUSINESS OR PLEASURE?—Julie Hogan
Daisy Kincaid quit her job when she realized that her boss, Alex Mackenzie,
would never reciprocate her feelings. But when the sexy CEO pleaded for
her to return and granted her a promotion to tempt her back, would the
new, unexpectedly close business-trip quarters finally turn their business
relationship into the pleasure she desired?

SDCNM0904